SEAFORTH

Hugh Miller was born in Scotland but has lived for more than twenty-five years in Warwickshire. He is the author of a number of books, among them the acclaimed Mike Fletcher crime novels and *The Silent Witnesses*, a study of the work of forensic pathologists. He also wrote the bestselling *Casualty*. His books have been translated into most Western languages.

Hugh Miller lives in Warwick with his wife, Nettie.

SEAFORTH

Hugh Miller

This edition published in Great Britain 1995 by
SEVERN HOUSE PUBLISHERS LTD of
9–15 High Street, Sutton, Surrey SM1 1DF.
by arrangement with the Pengu███████████Enterprises Ltd

British Library Cataloguing in Publication Data
Miller, Hugh
  Seaforth
  I. Title
  823.914 [F]

  ISBN 0-7278-4734-1

Typeset by Hewer Text Composition Services, Edinburgh.
Printed and bound in Great Britain by
Hartnolls Ltd, Bodmin, Cornwall.

I

Towards midnight the air raid siren started up. It sent people to the cupboards under the stairs and brought others from their houses, going towards the shelters in their slippers and nightclothes. At Mafeking Park on the poor side of the Yorkshire town of Seaforth a crowd hurried along Kitchener Street, past the Fishing Net chip shop, past Jacko's second-hand shop, heading for the shelter at the end of the road. Torch beams danced in the dark and children whined and grumbled: this had long ago stopped being fun.

The door at number 18 opened as the tail end of the crowd passed. Bob Longman put his head out and watched them, dim receding shapes as they moved on to cluster round the door of the shelter. He stood for a minute, liking the darkness close around him, feeling the dying tremor of the siren on the door panels, hearing it rattle the window frame. He ducked back inside, put on an ARP helmet and grabbed the sit-up-and-beg bike leaning against the wall.

He cycled along Kitchener Street in the middle of the road, hearing the whirr of the chain echo off the walls on either side. A man appeared at the kerb, running back from the shelter, hurrying to fetch something he'd forgotten.

'Get inside!' Bob yelled.

His voice sounded older in the dark. He could give it that heavy gruff tone of authority, especially if he tucked his chin nearer his neck when he spoke. He grinned, cycling harder, making the tyres hiss on the wet road.

Night time was his time. He could go from place to place without anybody staring and wondering. He could even pass himself off as an ARP warden. The raids and the darkness, combined, were good business. People left their houses, dropped everything – and obeyed the warden.

The siren finally died and the night went quiet again, only the sound of his tyres and his breath, the faint breeze in his ears as he pedalled through the lull before the bombers came. He passed out of Mafeking Park into a tidy, genteel new estate, looking to left and right, keeping to the warden's role even when nobody was watching. A part was only worth playing if you stayed inside it and played it to the hilt.

He could hear the drone of planes in the distance as he pedalled up the hill at Bank Top. The Victorian villas of the prosperous loomed on either side. These were forbidding places, weather-blackened strongholds of Yorkshire stone, ancient proofing against the winds that came across the moor, direct from the North Sea. The air felt colder here, like the people. Bob eased up off the saddle and put all his weight on the pedals for a couple of minutes, then he got off and pushed.

Flares in the distance were followed by a rumble, the first stick of bombs. Bob stopped for a second and

saw the faint orange glow to the south-east. Somebody'd get it. It was always Mafeking Park, never the
rich. Well, he'd make up for that in his small way.
Then there would be pickings in the bombed buildings.
It was an ill wind, as his mother said frequently.

He walked on a few yards and stopped before an
imposing gateway. The shape of the house was just
visible, a fraction darker than the sky behind it. He
compared it briefly with the rabbit hutch of a place he
lived in with his mother and his sisters and his brother.
He took a step along the entrance path, checking for
lights. Another bomb landed, nearer this time, making
the ground tremble. Better get on with it.

Upstairs in the big house Mark Winter, six months
old, was crying. Down in the kitchen the maid, Paula
Wickham, hurried about collecting his blankets and
his carry-cot for the shelter. Paula was aimless in her
haste, nervous and frightened by the bombs, anxiously
pushing back her long, red-brown hair. As she turned
up the gas under the kettle – she had to take in a
Thermos of tea – another bomb went off and she
heard the windows rattle.

Mark's mother, Penny, came down the wide stairs
carrying him. She was still half asleep, wearing a
sweater over her nightdress and an outdoor coat with a
WVS armband on the sleeve. She held out the baby and
as soon as Paula took him his crying softened. They
went to the kitchen, where the kettle was boiling. Penny
made straight for the big plump refrigerator and took
out a joint of ham. She put criss-crossing scrapes of
butter on a slice of bread and cut a piece from the joint.

'Mrs Scanlon has probably weighed and measured this,' she said, slapping the ham on the bread. 'But I woke up dreaming about it.'

She attacked the sandwich with adolescent heartiness. Penny was thirty, eleven years older than Paula, though for most of the time the gap seemed greater. Now, momentarily, the age difference narrowed as Penny gleefully bit into the bread and ham.

Her jaw froze for an instant as three overlapping explosions, alarmingly loud, brought down dust from the ceiling in a haze around the lampshade. The baby started to cry again. Paula held him close. The noise seemed to make Penny jubilant.

'Sounds like Mafeking Park,' she said, going to the window and peering through a chink at the side of the blackout. 'I should be down there. Just my luck.'

If it was possible to say anyone enjoyed the war, Penny Winter did. She wedged the rest of the sandwich in her mouth, took the baby from Paula, and pointed to a pile of WVS papers and folders on the side of the table.

'Bring those,' she mumbled, through the bread and ham. 'Come on, Mark . . .' She smiled at the baby. 'Let's go and hide from those nasty horrible men.'

She flung the door open and went out into the garden, picking her way to the Anderson shelter in the dim glow from the kitchen. Paula was at the table, pouring tea into the Thermos, when suddenly a whistle sounded, a piercing blast right outside the open door. She jumped. Tea shot past the mouth of the flask and made a steaming puddle on the table. Its edge crept towards the pile of papers. Paula put down the teapot and the flask and snatched the papers out of the way. In her alarm she knocked several of them into the puddle.

'Put out that light!' a gruff voice barked from outside. 'Get into the shelter!'

Paula dropped a tea-towel on the soaking papers, seized them with the others and ran out the door, slamming it shut behind her. She saw the shape of the warden as she hurried past him to the shelter. He said nothing and remained motionless, a helmeted monolith in the gloom.

Paula got to the shelter and eased herself inside. In the strange earth-smelling surroundings Mark had gone quiet, watching his mother and Paula with wide round eyes. Paula tucked him into his carry-cot and spoke softly to him, leaning close, cooing and murmuring until his eyes began to close.

Penny, fully awake now, was sorting the papers, spreading them across a tray on her knees. She was almost rubbing her hands. There was nothing she liked better than organizing, putting paper and people into order. Paula told her about the warden out in the garden.

'Little Hitler,' Penny said. 'I can just see it in his book!' She screwed up her face and did a whining impersonation: 'Light on in WVS District Organizer's. Warning given.' She picked up a damp sheaf of papers, thumbed through them and put them down, then rummaged through the others. She looked up, pouting like a child who discovers part of a game is missing.

'Where's the canteen forms, Paula? And the immuniza-
tion list?'

'Aren't they there?'

Penny searched, and shook her head.

'I must have left them,' Paula groaned. 'I was a bit
flustered, what with him and his whistle . . .'

'Go and get them,' Penny said, as if an air raid was
no impediment to a housemaid's movements. 'There's
your call-up deferment among them. I must do that for
you.'

'I . . . I wanted to talk to you about that, Mrs
Winter . . .'

'Oh, don't you worry about it, Paula,' Penny reas-
sured her while she scribbled. 'The idea of you joining
the forces is absurd. They know I'm doing an absolutely vital job and —'

'That's what I want to do!' Paula blurted, surprised
at herself but letting the impulse take her. 'A vital job!'

Penny looked up, sensing the tension. 'You are. Believe
me.' She smiled with careful precision. 'Aren't you?'

'Well, yes, yes, but —'

'I don't know what I'd do without you. I'll make
that absolutely clear to them. You are being wonderful
and I do appreciate that.'

Paula smiled at the praise. 'Well, thank you . . .' A
glow of pleasure settled on her frustration, all but
smothering it. But she struggled to keep to the point.
'Thank you, Mrs Winter, but . . .'

'Nip in and get the papers, will you?' Penny said
briskly. 'There's a good girl.'

*

When Bob had watched Paula hurry off to the shelter, and when he was sure she had gone inside, he went to the front of the house and tried the handle on the big door. It was locked. At the side of the house he tried the sash window of the reception room. It wouldn't budge. He stood for a minute, waiting, then as the sound of the bombing intensified he gripped the shaft of his torch and used the end of it to smash the window. He bashed away the broken pieces sticking to the frame and undid the catch. In less than a minute he was in the house.

He shone his torch around the room, seeing the glow of a mahogany sideboard, and in the window bay a desk. On it were two photographs – one a smiling young woman, pretty and rather haughty-looking, the other a handsome, serious-looking man in a military officer's uniform – in elegant silver frames. The sight of the frames was like the turning of an emotional key, a sweet movement in his stomach. He knew what he could get rid of and could almost immediately translate it into money.

He played the torch about the walls, looking for the light switch, and saw his face in the mirror above the mantelpiece. He liked what he saw, lit dimly and dramatically in reflected light from the wall. He smiled at the mirror. A great smile, engaging, sincere when he wanted it to be. He could translate that into money too.

He had no option. He was nine months over the call-up age. His father was dead, and his mother was a drunk. How would the family survive without him?

Well, that was his story and it was mostly true. He also felt — somehow — that he and the Army wouldn't get on. Without a ration book or an identity card he had to earn his living as a rather unconventional ARP warden.

He put on the light, went to the desk and slipped the silver frames into his pocket. At the sideboard he opened both big drawers and fingered through the contents, always hopeful of finding cash. Nothing.

He put out the light and went to the hall. At the foot of the stairs he paused, seeing light under a door. He opened it cautiously and peered in. It was the kitchen where he had seen the girl pouring tea into a flask. He grinned. She had shot away quickly enough.

He went in soundlessly and closed the door behind him. For a minute he stood still, taking it in. They didn't know what life was all about here. A mouse, he had often said, could starve trying to find a spare crumb in the Longman house. Here, food was lying wherever he looked. He saw jam, fresh-looking bread, a small block of butter, a wedge of cheese . . .

His heart leapt when he saw the ham. He had never seen meat like it out of a shop. His mouth ran with saliva. He strode across the room and picked it up, sniffed it and took the smell deep into his lungs. The door opened and Paula walked in.

For a moment Bob looked as if he would throw the ham at her. Then he saw how frightened she was, and how pretty. She was pale, her hair glinting auburn and gold in the overhead light. In a flash he absorbed the look of her, the set of her face: she had a quality of eyes and mouth that drew him, a frank clear stare and a hesitating look about her lips. Her breathing was nervous, he could hear it from where he stood, clutching the ham. He put on his smile – not his engaging, but his wavery, poverty-stricken smile.

'I was only going to take a slice,' he said.

'Put it down.'

He laid the joint carefully on the table. Obedience and humility, he calculated, would work best there. Paula turned back to the door.

'Please don't tell her,' he said, making his voice throaty and compliant, watching Paula take confidence from that. She stared contemptuously at his helmet. He lowered his eyes. 'I'm sorry. It's just that I haven't had anything today, and I ...' He looked up again. 'I've never done it before, Miss, honest I haven't.'

The first wave of bombers had passed and in the relative quiet Penny could be heard calling to Paula. That irritated Paula, Bob could sense that. Was he in with a chance? He stared at her, his eyes beseeching. Paula glared back at him, entwining her fingers, twisting them.

'Get out.'

'Oh, thank you,' he said, adding a little gulp to underline his gratitude. 'Thanks, Miss. I won't ever do it again.'

Penny called louder. Paula glanced in the direction of her voice. 'Coming!' she shouted, anger in her voice. She picked up the ham as Bob made for the door. 'Here.'

He watched, fascinated, as she took a knife and cut

off a thick slice of the ham. She was a really easy touch this one. He let his lips quiver and his eyes stare hopefully. 'I've a brother and two sisters,' he said.

He thought he'd gone too far, but Paula cut off another slice. The picture became clearer. He knew servility when he saw it.

'You're the servant,' he murmured.

'*Personal* maid,' she snapped.

As she came forward to give him the ham there was an ear-splitting bang. It happened so fast there was no time to understand or respond. The room had disappeared in a cloud of plaster. Bob staggered back, covered in it, seeing the wall opposite melt and sway towards him and stop, held up by a fallen beam. His ears were battered by waves and waves of noise.

The beam gave way with a crack and the wall fell inwards. Bob jerked back and nearly trod on Paula. Her mouth was open but he couldn't hear her screaming. Her dress was ripped, her arms cut and bleeding. More plaster showered down on them. Bob turned to make a run for the one open space he could see and Paula grabbed him. He tried to shake her off but her grip tightened. Did he really help her out of the wreckage or was she clinging on to him?

Outside Penny was running from the shelter in her bare feet. At the sight of an entire wing of the house half destroyed and burning she stopped, appalled.

'God forgive me, God forgive me . . .'

As she stared, a man came staggering out of the smoke towards her. It was like the enactment of a miracle. He was a warden, and he was supporting

Paula, half dragging, half carrying her over the rubble as she clung to him. Penny ran forward into the smoke, coughing, ignoring the pain in her bleeding feet, stretching her hands out to Paula. She drew the girl into her arms and hugged her, rocking her from side to side.

'Paula, Paula ...' She smoothed the hair from Paula's face and saw her eyes flicker open. 'Oh, thank God, thank –'

With a roar that made the ground shake the remaining walls and timbers of the kitchen caved in. Penny scurried back, dragging Paula, stumbling away from the choking clouds of smoke and dust. When she could feel cool air on her face she stopped and blinked the stinging dust from her eyes. She looked about her and realized, vaguely, that the warden had disappeared.

2

'He saves her life,' Mrs Wickham said, her voice incredulous, 'and she can't remember what he looks like.'

She stood in the doorway between the lounge and the hall, aproned and with a duster in her hand. She was a spare-figured woman in her fifties, of fastidious, almost manic cleanliness. She had spent that morning giving the house an extra-thorough cleaning, sensing that the air raid had caused an invisible skein of disorder to fall on her furniture and carpets. She firmly believed a good dust and polish always put things right, or at least, as right as possible in this life.

'You can't remember? It's beyond me,' she said.

'He looked like Tyrone Power, mother.'

Paula was stretched out on the settee, her scratches and bruises livid in the daylight, although she was not injured to any serious extent. Even so, she was making the most of the opportunity to have time off. She frowned at her mother and pictured again the boy, well, he was a young man really, with his sharp features and dark eyes. He could have been quite handsome if he hadn't whined so much. She could have admitted that his face was the first thing that came into her mind when she woke up, but she didn't.

'I was unconscious.'

'That's not unusual,' Mrs Wickham said tartly. 'You have to be unconscious to even think of leaving Mrs Winter.'

'Mother, please!'

At the table Paula's boyfriend, Richard, was repairing a wireless set. He was a tidy-looking airman of twenty-three in a groundstaff uniform, a quiet-natured, fastidious person Paula had known since childhood. If Richard had one notable characteristic it was his tendency, occasionally, to frown cautiously before he smiled; to Richard life was an experience which demanded to be understood, rather than something to which he should simply respond. Sitting in the strong light from the front room window, his Brylcreemed head bowed and bobbing gently as he worked on the radio, he was oblivious to the exchange between Paula and her mother.

'I'm not saying a word,' Mrs Wickham said, absently polishing the back of the couch with her duster, 'but a job like that, living in, all found, doesn't grow on trees.'

Paula turned her head aside in the careful, languishing way of someone too sick to argue. Mrs Wickham sighed and went out, shutting the door. Paula sat up at once.

'I feel so left out, Richard!' Paula slapped the side of the settee to get his full attention. 'I want to *do* something!'

The wireless crackled and Richard grunted, nodding at it as he made an adjustment.

'Could I be a radar plotter?' Paula asked him. 'Like Jenny?'

Richard looked at her for a moment. 'You need school certificates.' The wireless lit up and hummed. He grunted again.

'How did you get leave so quickly?'

'Compassionate,' he said.

'What?'

'I said I were . . .' Orchestral music suddenly came over the wireless at full volume. Richard pulled away a wire and it fell silent again. 'That's it!' He twirled the end of the wire. 'A bit of solder'll do it.'

'You said you were what?'

'Engaged,' Richard said.

They looked at one another. Paula was shocked.

'You shouldn't have said that!'

'No. I know. I . . .' Richard frowned. 'I – I'm sorry. I was really worried about you and it was the only way I could . . .'

He broke off. They looked at one another again. The telephone in the hall rang. They heard Mrs Wickham answer it.

'Don't be daft,' Paula said. 'I mean I can't remember a time when I didn't know you and I suppose . . . we are . . . are we?'

'Are we?' Richard's ears coloured slightly. 'If –' He cleared his throat, started again, trying to align his thoughts. 'Do you, I mean, want to?'

Paula jumped off the settee and kissed him. Of course they were engaged! They always had been! They separated abruptly as the door opened.

'The *Seaforth Gazette*,' Mrs '
'About your bomb.'
'My – *what*?' Paula starte
said. 'Mother, we're . . .'
Mrs Wickham picked up the te.
caller Paula was ill.
'Mo-*ther*!'
Paula went to the hall. Her mother held ou.
receiver and waited, expressionless, while Paula
checked her hair in the mirror before answering it.

Mafeking Park was the poorest region of Seaforth.
The area was mainly rows of red brick terraced houses,
two up and two down, with long narrow passages –
which people called ginnels – connecting the tops of
the terraces.

In one such ginnel, on the morning after the air raid,
at roughly the time Paula Wickham was giving her
story to the reporter from the *Seaforth Gazette*, three
small boys sat cross-legged on the ground, quarrelling
over a cigarette-cards swap. One of them, a thin-
cheeked, large-eyed eight-year-old called Brian Longman, known to everyone as Bri, happened to look up
and saw an Army jeep pull in at the far end of the
ginnel. Looking the other way, behind him, he saw a
second jeep draw up. A number of Redcaps jumped
out.

Bri had got to the point in the argument where he
had agreed to swop two Herbert Sutcliffe cricket cards
for one Len Hutton. He had been trying to get Len for
weeks and had finally done so. But he was so distracted

ght of the Redcaps that he forgot Len, dropped
d ran through the ginnel. Skinny knees pumping
sly, he ran to 18 Kitchener Street, where he took
uple of gulps of breath before yanking his mouth
to piercing whistles aimed at the upstairs window.

Bob was asleep in the room he shared with Bri. He
stirred and twitched as the second whistle splintered
his sleep. He opened an eye slowly. Morning light
through the thin curtain made stripes across Bri's
Daily Mirror war maps stuck on the wall over the bed.
The motionless air smelt of warm bodies and stale
clothing.

The third whistle made him sit up. He swung his
feet over the side of the bed, grabbing his shirt and the
ARP helmet, and stuck his feet in his boots. He bolted
out of the room wearing the unbuttoned shirt, his
underpants and boots, with his trousers clutched in
one hand and the helmet in the other. On the way to
the front door he lost the trousers and ran out into the
street still carrying the helmet. He bolted for the row
of lavatories marked 18–20–22 and disappeared
through the street door in front of them.

He leaned on the other side of the door for a
second, panting, hearing the distant sound of boots.
Two Redcaps were marching along Kitchener Street
with a couple of small boys strutting behind, imitating
them.

Bob tried a cubicle door. It was bolted. He tried the
next one and it stuck. He kicked it and it flew open.
There was an indignant squawk and he had a glimpse
of a seated woman with voluminous knickers round

her ankles. He backed away as the door banged shut. At the street door he opened it a crack and peered out. The Redcaps were in front of number 18, one of them banging the thin door with the side of his fist.

Inside, Sal Longman was picking up the trousers Bob had lost on his way out. She was a red-faced, puffy-eyed woman in her forties, as slow-moving in a crisis as at other times. She had a habit of swivelling her eyes to look at people or objects a moment before her head turned in their direction. Wheezing now from the unaccustomed effort, she slung Bob's trousers on the trestle over the iron range beside clothes hung there to dry, then stood and looked for other signs of incrimination in the bare, drab room.

The banging at the door did not visibly disturb her. With the air of someone about to welcome guests, she touched a hand to her dark brown hair, which had been pinned up in the same untidy, impromptu style for so long it looked solid and artificial. At her side young Dora, five, clung close to her, a thumb plugged firmly in her mouth.

'Vera,' Sal said, 'there's someone at the door, love.'

Vera sat at the table in a boiler suit and turban, knitting while she read a book lying open on the oilcloth. She was nineteen, boyish-faced and sullen. When her mother spoke she stopped knitting, but only to turn a page. Sal answered the door herself.

From his position by the lavatories Bob saw the door at number 18 open and the Redcaps go in. Bob promptly ran shirt-tailed across the street to the lavatory entrance marked 41–43–45, found an empty cubicle and slipped inside. He banged the door shut and leaned on it, panting with his exertions but forcing himself to take shallow breaths, as he always did in the lavvies. He put his ear to the door, straining to hear sounds from the street, trying to ignore the stink issuing from the gaping hole in the plank seat behind him.

At number 18 Sal was putting on a close-to-tears benefit performance for the Redcaps, twisting her grease-blackened apron between her hands. Like her son, she could switch from one role to another – no doubt where he had got it from. The long-suffering mother was an old stand-by. At the mention of Bob's name she emitted a fag-rattle of a sigh and turned reddened eyes on her visitors.

'I wish I knew where he was,' she said, dabbing her nose with her apron. 'When they're babbies they break your arms, but when they grow up they break your heart. Isn't that right, Vera?'

Vera, who only needed to hear the tone of voice to stop listening to the words, continued to knit. One of the Redcaps pulled the trousers off the trestle and held them up. He looked down at young Bri.

'A bit big for you, aren't they, lad?'

'Poor Bri always has the cast-offs,' Sal said, making even the incriminating trousers into a plea for sympathy.

The Redcap picked up little Dora and held her in the crook of his arm. He smiled at her and she shyly smiled back.

'Have you seen your big brother, love?' he said.

'Yeh,' Dora said, nodding.

The Redcap smiled encouragingly, wrinkling his nose at the child. 'When?' he said.

Sal closed her eyes. She could have been making a swift prayer. In spite of all her effort, it looked as if she'd lost this one – or Bob had.

'I saw him before he left to go in the Army,' Dora said.

The Redcap's smile vanished. He put the child down. Sal beamed at him. Dora might not understand what she was saying, but she said it like a true Longman.

The third and fourth Redcaps were meanwhile heading for the lavatories marked 18–20–22. From his position in the cubicle Bob listened, picturing the soldiers' progress from the strident clacking of their boots and the banging of flimsy doors. He heard a woman screech, the same one as before, followed by the scuttering retreat of boots. Bob laughed, then swallowed it when he realized the boots were coming his way.

He leaned forward and peered through a crack. At the gap under the street door he saw shiny toecaps and watched them shift one way then the other as the Redcap looked about him. There was a shout from down the street; one of the Redcaps who had gone into the house, Bob presumed, was reporting to his mates. 'The bastard's done a bunk. Let's get out of it.'

He watched the boots turn around and walk away. Seconds later a jeep started up, then another, and drove off. In defiance of the atmosphere Bob took a deep breath and let it out slowly. *Hallelujah*, he thought, and shivered, realizing for the first time how cold he was. He could go home now and get his trousers on just as soon as he completed urgent business in that dank little stall.

3

At the Winter household the business of clearing up was accomplished swiftly; life was firmly manoeuvred back to normal. An entire wing of the house had been destroyed, but there was plenty of room elsewhere. On Paula's return to work she found Penny Winter as buoyant as ever, coping, administering and – unbelievably – enjoying it.

Paula found Penny's enjoyment depressing. She had to get out and *do* something. What, she had no idea, except that she was sick of being a servant. She had to speak to Penny again. The main problem was how to get a word in edgeways.

How on earth did Penny do it? Paula could only watch helplessly and be jealous. By mid-morning, negotiations and finely-balanced arguments had established a deal between Penny and the council. In exchange for metal scrap from the ruined wing of the house, the council would guarantee a few hours' work by maintenance employees to clear a decent path to the door at the west side of the house. Penny, pleased with herself, decided she had earned a treat. She sat down at the desk in the reception room with a cup of tea, and wrote to her husband, Colonel Andrew Winter.

She told him about the bomb with zest. It was a

long letter, and as she felt it was her duty to inspire him, she ended by describing how Paula had been saved from death by an ARP warden. 'I'm sure, Andrew, darling,' she wrote, 'you would be proud of such a man in your regiment . . .'

She looked up, gazing at the place where the silver-framed photographs had been. Paula was clearing away a tray. Penny asked her if the pictures had shown up yet.

'No, Mrs Winter.'

'Funny . . .'

The room had not been hit, although the windows had been broken. The frames were the only things missing.

Paula was picking up a glass when a thought struck her. She froze, seeing his face again, remembering his bulging pockets. The glass slipped from her fingers and smashed on the floor.

Penny stared at her. 'What are you doing?' Paula still looked distant, troubled. 'What's the matter? What's wrong?'

'I've just remembered.'

'What?'

Paula's tongue flicked across her lips. 'I was just remembering – that night, what happened.'

Penny nodded. 'Try not to dwell on it,' she said with an understanding frown. 'That was rather a nice glass.'

'I'm sorry.'

'Go and lie down for a bit.' Penny went back to her letter, nodding at the fragments on the floor. 'When you've cleared that up,' she added.

That evening, flush with the cash Jacko had given him for the picture frames, Bob went along to the Fishing Net with Bri. The place was crowded as usual at that time of night and they had to queue in the steamy interior, Bri passing the time drawing pictures in the steam on the green-painted walls.

When it was their turn they ordered fish and chips for five, with extra chips and, at Bri's special request, an extra scoop of batter scraps. As they waited for Webb, the proprietor, to shovel the chips on to the squares of paper, Bob did a well-rehearsed George Raft impersonation, flipping a half-crown in the air and catching it, over and over again.

Behind them in the queue was Fred Spence, a foreman at Winter's Engineering Works and the father of Bob's pal Arthur, who was now in the Army. Behind Fred two women, Mrs Thomas and Miss Thwaites, were talking about Bob. Fred Spence had been reading his *Seaforth Gazette*, but now he absently laid it on the counter as he listened to what the women were saying. Bob caught a glimpse of the front page and stopped flipping his coin. He stared at the paper, transfixed.

'I must say,' murmured Mrs Thomas, who was always keen to see the best side of people, 'he does provide for the family. I don't know where he gets it from.'

They watched Bob gather up his parcel from the counter and give it an extra wrap before he and Bri left the shop, cheerily calling goodnight to Webb.

'He gets it from the same place as his father, no doubt,' said Miss Thwaites, her lips seeming to cling to the front of her teeth as she spoke. 'And you know what happened to him. He would have hanged if he hadn't had the good fortune to die in prison.'

Fred Spence entered the discussion. 'If it weren't for his being our Arthur's mucker,' he said, 'I'd turn him in myself.'

Mrs Thomas nodded. Miss Thwaites sniffed. Fred turned back to the counter. He frowned.

'Where's my paper?' he demanded.

Further along Kitchener Street Bob had stopped by a thin shaft of light slanting from the edge of a blackout curtain. He peeled Fred Spence's newspaper from around the warm fat parcel, which he handed to Bri. He held the paper into the slim shaft of light and stared at the picture of Paula Wickham under the headline

MYSTERY OF THE MODEST HERO

Rescues Woman – Then Disappears

When they finally got back to number 18 there was jubilation as the fish and chips, still in their paper, were put to warm on the range. Dora and Bri ran round chanting 'A feast! A feast!' while Sal made a pot of tea.

Vera did not look so pleased as the others. For one thing she was preoccupied: she had lost her purse, which she normally kept in her sewing basket. For a young girl Vera had a strong sense of order and an unyielding belief that a person's belongings, however poor and few, should be respected. Bob, she knew, had nothing to do with the disappearance of her purse – he wouldn't even borrow without asking. Nevertheless she watched him stonily as he sat down with the others to dig into the meal. It was her way of showing her disapproval of the means he had used – whatever they were this time – to buy them such a slap-up meal.

'Don't worry,' he finally told her. 'I found . . .'

'. . . something on a bomb site,' Vera finished for him.

He put on a face of bright amazement. 'How did you guess?' He took the folded-up *Seaforth Gazette* from his pocket and handed it to her. 'Could you read this?' She took the paper from him, unfolding it. 'I've lost my glasses,' he added flippantly.

Between them the family took less than ten minutes to eat every scrap. When the meal was over they sat around the table, their mouths and chins shining with grease. Vera spread the *Gazette* on the table before her and read the front-page story aloud. She delivered the dramatic details well, putting emotion into her voice as she read the reporter's florid description of how the ARP warden, a true man of mystery, had dragged the housemaid from an otherwise certain death in a bombed and tumbling wing of the home of Colonel and Mrs Andrew Winter.

'"He seemed to come from nowhere, and then vanish. It was like a miracle," said Paula Wickham of Moorland Road, Albany Gardens. "I owe my life to him." Mrs Winter, whose family runs the big engineering firm, added, "His modesty makes us even more keen to thank him."'

Vera pushed the paper away. Sal was moist-eyed as she fished out a Park Drive and lit it.

'Wonderful,' she said. 'Makes your heart feel good, doesn't it, that there are folk like that in this evil world.'

Bob looked across the table at her. 'What would you say if it were me?'

She stared back at him. 'Say? I'd be bloody flabbergasted you hadn't already been up there to claim the reward!'

The others laughed.

'Reward?' Bob said, his face very serious now.

More laughter, and Bri thumped the table.

'I wouldn't try it, lad,' Sal said. 'Knowing you, you'd turn up at same time as real bloke.'

During the afternoon young Mark Winter had suffered an upset stomach. It was better now, but his timetable had been disturbed and by eight o'clock he was still not asleep. Paula walked backwards and forwards across the landing outside his room with him cradled in her arms, rocking him, humming softly, willing him to close his eyes and drift off. She could hear Penny downstairs in the hall, talking on the telephone.

'He's bright as a button,' she said. 'I'm fine, except that I don't know what I'll do if I lose Paula . . .'

At the mention of her name Paula moved softly to the top of the stairs. The baby, who had been falling asleep, stirred at the change in rhythm. Paula stood still with him, swinging from side to side, straining to hear.

'That wretched man at the Ministry has turned down my request to keep her! With the number of hours I do at the WVS I'm entitled to ... What? ... Oh, Paula doesn't know yet, she'll probably fall to pieces when I ...'

The baby cried out, a solitary abrupt high note. Paula turned away sharply and walked into the bedroom. In the hall Penny stepped back as far as the telephone cable permitted and bent over to look up the stairs. She straightened again and apologized to her caller, explaining that she had thought Paula was in the vicinity.

'I'll have another go at the Ministry man, but these officials can be so obstinate, especially nowadays when they've got so much power.'

Upstairs Paula was no longer coercing the baby into sleep. Instead she marched back and forth, saluting him as she sang, in a soft jubilant whisper, 'I'm joining up! I'm joining up!'

The baby chuckled with pure delight. The ripple of diversion seemed to be just the thing needed to soothe him, for five minutes later he was fast asleep. Paula tucked him in, went to her own room and put on her outdoor coat. She slipped a torch into her pocket and went downstairs, telling Penny she was going to look in on her mother, as she did a couple of times a week.

She went through the Memorial Park, down towards the town. She thought she heard someone and the park made her nervous. She hurried, keeping her torch beam pointed at the ground. As she approached the wide flight of steps at the far end, her pace slackened. By peering through the dark she could just make out the reassuring sandbagged shape of the ARP post ahead of her, a few yards beyond the foot of the steps.

Then she stiffened, hearing footsteps close by. They came nearer and she started moving towards the steps, going as fast as she could, fixing her eyes on the ARP post. She was aware that the other person was close behind, following her to the top of the steps. The torch beam danced ahead of her, lighting up edges, creating shadows, confusing her. She glanced aside and saw a man, two feet away. She stumbled and the man caught her. With a small gasp she found herself looking into Bob's face.

Angrily she pulled her arm free and hurried on ahead of him. He followed her again. She stopped and stared back at him.

'How dare you come back!' she snapped.

'You wanted to see me!' Bob said. 'To thank me! The newspaper said!'

'I had to say that! I couldn't say . . .' she gestured dismissively. 'I don't know what came over me. I couldn't say you were a thief.'

'I'm not a thief!'

Paula brought the torch up at him as if it were a weapon. 'You broke in!'

'I was hungry!'

'Did you take anything else?'

'What?' His face stiffened with wounded innocence. 'No, of course I didn't!'

The intensity of the denial shook Paula's certainty. So did the next thing he said.

'Come for a drink,' he said quickly. 'To the Blue.'

He moved towards her and she brought up the torch defensively.

'Keep that torch down!' a warden shouted.

Bob put his hand over the torch to point it to the ground. Paula, mistaking his intention, tried to jerk it away from him.

'Keep it down!'

The clash of movements created a confused moment between them, and then the torch fell to the ground. In the darkness Paula panicked.

'Help!' she shouted 'Help!'

'You bloody tart!' Bob roared. 'You said –'

He heard the warden running towards them and ran off into the bushes. The warden reached Paula, who was shakily trying to find her torch.

'Are you all right, Miss? I'll phone the police from the post. Did you get a good look at him?'

Paula stared at the man. For a few seconds she scarcely breathed and simply stood there trembling, her mind racing. She ought to tell him. She very nearly did. The warden – the real warden – with his accusing helmet, stared at her. She had certainly taken a good look at him. Several good looks: she could accurately describe him, and she knew he was a thief who drank at the Blue, wherever that was. She opened her mouth to tell him, but somehow the words would not come out.

'Did you see his face?' the warden repeated.

'No,' she said. 'I didn't.'

4

The way Bob woke up suggested he had been switched on. There was no gradual surfacing, no reluctance to face the day. He was quite simply asleep one minute, awake the next. He lay looking at the ceiling, aware of the intrusion of cold truth.

Last night, listening to Vera read from the paper, he had known that the person they told about, the non-existent hero, was nevertheless a definite possibility, a gallant, enigmatic natural success that he, Bob Long-man, could easily become. It was just a matter of wanting to be that person badly enough. And the understanding had put strength in a notion that was dear to him, that he could work at being just whoever he wanted to be, and manage it. The possibilities within such a talent were without end.

Now, after what had happened in the park, after the demonstration that some features of his luck stuck to him like dogshit on his heel, he felt the chill of truth, although he wanted to believe it wasn't the truth for ever after, but just the truth *for now*. And the truth, quite simply, was what he had read in her eyes: that he was a shit and a thief on the run. So what – so bloody what!

'It was *here*!' he heard Vera shouting downstairs. 'I put it here!'

Bob's eyes roamed the patchy ceiling and down along the wall. Among Bri's newspaper war maps was the *Seaforth Gazette* with that cow's picture on the front and the story about the mystery man. He sat up sharply and tore the paper off the wall, balled it up and threw it into the corner. He got out of bed and stood by the window, groaning softly, stretching.

Downstairs Vera, wearing her turban, was holding her work basket and glaring at little Dora, who looked scared. Standing by the table in his shiny fifty-bob suit was Mr Thrush, the rent collector, a thin, sour-mouthed man who had lived through countless scenes like this. His Homburg hat was on the table and he held an open ledger and a pen.

'What happened to it, Dora?' Vera demanded.

'I don't know!' the child cried.

In a voice flat and empty of hope, Mr Thrush asked if it would help if he called back later.

'I'll be at work,' Vera said. 'The money's here.'

'But not here, Miss Longman.' Mr Thrush tapped his book. 'You promised you wouldn't fall behind another week. I'm afraid . . .' He shook his head ominously.

'I'll bring you it,' Bob said as he came into the room, buckling his belt.

'It's not my money,' Mr Thrush protested. 'I get it in the neck if I don't collect.'

Bob picked up the Homburg and held it out to Mr Thrush. Thrush looked at Bob carefully then took the hat. He left without another word. You didn't spend as much time as he did in Mafeking Park without learning what should be avoided, and when.

Bob turned to Vera as the door closed. 'Where is she?' He saw that Dora was dipping a liquorice stick into the remains of a sherbet fountain. He snatched it from her. 'Did she buy you that?' he said. 'Where is she?'

Dora began to cry.

'Bob,' Vera said, 'don't . . .'

'You get off, Vera!' he shouted.

The front door banged open and Bri stood in the opening, panting. 'She's in the Blue,' he announced. 'They had a delivery of beer dinnertime.'

At that moment in the Blue Anchor, Miss Thwaites was staring with open dislike at Sal Longman as she flirted with a couple of American soldiers called Earl and Joe. Miss Thwaites was expressing a dislike that was many years old and, by now, habitual. Her underlying displeasure, one of many, was that the war had changed the once cosy, gossipy atmosphere of the pub to such an extent that she had to wonder if anything was sacred any more.

Nowadays the Blue Anchor was more popular than it had ever been. In the words of one of the regulars, it was somewhere nice and grubby and safe to crawl to in a world that had turned bloody dangerous. The licensee, Dick Moxham, concurred with that. He believed that as his pub stood, drabness and all, it was nothing less than a haven. And it was no dirtier than other havens of its kind in the district: 'It's not muck, anyway, it's character.' Films of nicotine tar on the light-bulbs and windows meant the place had a warm umber tint, an earthy colour intensified by older, time-hardened layers of tobacco smoke on the walls and ceiling.

The Blue managed to be a spacious place, too, in a cramped way, just right for occasional outbursts of public rejoicing when bombs missed their targets or when brewers managed to deliver extra quotas. In earlier days there had been a semi-genteel 'family' bar on one side and a public bar on the other. Now one public bar faced another across a space bounded by two counters, behind which Dick Moxham and his barmaid, Sue, served when there was beer enough to go round. Today there was more than enough.

'Another glass,' Sal promised, 'and I'll do my Gracie Fields.'

Groans of 'No, no' and pleas for mercy came from people scattered about the bar.

'There you are,' Sal said triumphantly, 'my fans.'

She swallowed the dregs from her glass, took up a singer's stance, and began singing 'We'll Meet Again'. The landlord came across. He took Sal's arm and whispered in her ear. She angled her head away from him, glaring stagily.

'Enough? I am stone-cold sober, Dick Moxham. You can't even get merry on the piss you serve here.'

That brought laughter and a few faint cheers. Sal flicked her skirts at Earl, took his glass and held it high.

'We're right behind you, Winnie!' she cried.

'Aye,' Miss Thwaites nodded, glowering from the opposite bar. 'Far behind.'

Outraged virtue churned across Sal's face. 'I've done my bit, Jessica Thwaites.'

'Drunk it, more like.'

'I've had six and raised four –'

'It's how you've raised them,' Miss Thwaites said, bile in her voice.

Bob came into the bar as Sal pushed her face threateningly into Miss Thwaites's and said, 'You couldn't even raise a man's – interest.'

People, like a ring round two boxers, burst out laughing. Miss Thwaites, red-faced and furious, pointed a stiff, shaking finger at Bob.

'Look at him,' she cried. 'There are lads out there dying while he –'

Her expression changed as she watched Bob walk up behind his mother and grab her by the arm. The surprise, combined with Bob's strength, meant Sal was at the door before she knew it.

'Leave off, will you!' She struggled and writhed and managed to wedge herself in the doorway. 'Why don't you go and fight instead of fighting your own mother!'

Bob persisted, pushing her forward in jerks until she was out on the pavement. He kept a tight grip on her arm and marched along the street with her, dragging her when she stumbled, forcing her to walk at his pace.

'Showing me up in front of that cow,' Sal snarled, weaving and stumbling after him. 'You pretend it's because of me but it's because you're bloody frightened. You're a bloody coward. You know that, don't you? A bloody coward. Well the next time they come I'll bloody well shop you –'

Bob stopped suddenly. He slammed her viciously

against the wall with such force it knocked the breath from her. She doubled over, wheezing, trying to breathe as he stood in front of her, his hands gripping the lapels of her coat.

'How can I leave?' he yelled, shaking her. 'How can I go back to the Army? How can I get a bloody job if I'm a deserter? How can I be anything when you're like this? How can I? *How can I?*'

Three minutes later Bri and little Dora were startled by the front door flying open and their mother staggering in. Bob was close behind her. He slammed the door shut.

'Hello, love,' Sal said, smiling lopsidedly at Dora. 'Just been having my sherbet.'

Dora backed away from her. Bob told the young ones to get upstairs. They went half-way up the stairs then stopped, watching. Bob didn't notice. His anger had got to the point where he could hardly control it. He stepped up to his mother.

'I told you,' he said.

She shook her head. 'No. No.' She backed away.

'I told you, Mother.' He followed her round the table. 'I told you.'

'No, Bob. Please. I promise . . .'

'You promised afore and afore and afore and afore!' He smashed his fist on the table with each word. Sal screamed and lashed out at him, clawing his cheek. He caught her by the arms and pinned her down. 'I swore I would and I will! I will!'

The children watched in a strange combination of fear and fascination as Bob gripped Sal's left hand

35

and tried to pull off her wedding ring. She struggled and yelled and kicked at him.

'It won't come off!' she screamed.

'Right!' Bob yanked open a drawer in the table. 'Then I'll cut the bugger off!'

Knives and forks jangled out on to the floor. He seized a knife. Sal was incoherent with terror. She struggled to break away from him, shuddering with fright, trying to drag the ring down over her knuckle. Bob flung the knife aside and snatched the ring off her finger. Sal screamed as a slice of skin went with it.

'Bob,' she wailed, clutching her hand, 'it's all I've got left.'

He saw the blood on her hand and compassion overwhelmed him suddenly. 'Mother, Mother . . .' He drew her close to him. 'I told you. I told you.'

She reached out suddenly and tried to snatch the ring back. Bob shoved her away violently and ran from the house. He could pop the ring for at least a pound at Jacko's. That would pay off the rent, and maybe leave enough for a drink.

'Excellent news, Paula!' Penny called, coming in through the front door.

Paula turned from the window, startled. She had been making up a bottle for Mark and had slipped into a daydream, staring through the window into the garden. She had been picturing what it would be like, being her own woman.

She was in the makeshift kitchen which had been set up in a corner of the reception room. A plumber had been persuaded to re-route a cold water pipe and fit it with a tap, which let into an old sink that had lain for years in a potting shed doing nothing. A length of pipe, furtively commandeered from the pile of metal set aside for the council scrap yard, served as a drain pipe which actually led to a real drain at the side of the house. Shelves, small cupboards and an old dresser had been pushed into place by Penny and Paula. Penny had decided that with determination, the arrangement would work very well.

She came in now, beaming, looking sprucely efficient in her WVS uniform and carrying her briefcase. She repeated that she had excellent news, in case Paula hadn't heard her.

'I've fixed it,' she said. 'You're staying with me!'

Paula stared at her. 'But Mrs Winter, I want to —'

'Isn't that wonderful? Now we can all —'

'I want to join up!' Paula shouted. Suddenly her hands were trembling.

Penny blinked at her. 'Why on earth didn't you say so before?'

'I did. I tried.' Paula shook her head, making an effort to explain herself lucidly. 'I heard you saying you couldn't get me off, so I thought . . .'

Penny put down her briefcase, visibly choking back a retort, making a change of gear. 'Mark would miss you,' she said.

'I know. I'll miss him.'

'And I've been working so hard to keep you.'

'I know.' Paula shrugged. 'I am sorry.'

'So am I,' Penny said wryly. 'The thing is, I don't

know if I can do anything about it now. It's all been arranged.'

Paula wrapped her hands around the teapot and raised it an inch. She could easily have flung it through the window with frustration.

'Are you absolutely sure, Paula?'

Indecision began to close in. Paula took a small step back, an instinctive avoiding action. Penny watched her, gauging her strength.

'Yes, of course, I . . .'

Penny saw what was happening. She could detect a flimsy will almost without trying. She smiled, becoming more decisive, driving a spike at Paula's wavering.

'Why don't you take the evening off?' she suggested. 'Talk to your mother. Will you promise me you'll do that?'

Paula wanted to say *no, no, I won't, just leave me* . . . but she nodded, hating her own decency, loathing her capacity for accommodating this woman whenever she turned on the pressure.

'I promise,' she said.

5

Bob rested his face on cold stonework and stood stock-still, blending with the architecture as someone walked past on the pavement, ten feet away. It was cold again, not quite dark yet, the kind of night when he would have been happy to sit in the Blue enjoying a drink and the noise of other people, or cuddling up alongside young Sue with her sausage curls and her plucked eyebrows and her marvellous scarlet bow lips.

But Jacko, the tight bastard, had refused to offer him more than eighteen shillings on the ring. Bob needed a pound at the very least, but Jacko was immovable. He already had a trayful of wedding and engagement rings among the unredeemed pledges in his wire-grilled window. Eighteen shillings was his last word. He could neither satisfy the rent man, nor his own thirst.

So Bob was here, three houses down from the Winters' place, preparing to force the catch on a side window. He had made a promise to Thrush and that promise was one of the kind he kept, no matter what.

He swore as his hand slipped and his knuckles raked across stone. Changing angle, he leaned on the catch then froze as another set of footsteps approached. He put his face to the wall again, watching the pavement, and was astonished to see the maid – sorry, *personal* maid – go past.

He moved away from the window, wondering if he was being given signals by some power beyond, then promptly wondering at his capacity to kid himself. Even so . . .

He went to the gate and looked down the hill, seeing Paula dimly in the failing light, her flowing hair and her strong, positive step unmistakable. Where the hell was she going? Across the park. Into the darkness. Going south. Down the steps. Silently he followed her. Wasn't there something about her movements now that was quiet, furtive, like his own?

Ten minutes later, Paula stood staring at the rows of back-to-back houses at Mafeking Park. She walked along one street to the very end, ducking under lines of washing still hanging there, and looked across a bomb site towards the Blue Anchor. As she watched, the American soldiers Earl and Joe made their way along the road and entered the pub. She turned away sharply and found herself staring straight into Bob's face. Again.

'Where are you going?' he asked her.

'Just walking,' she said, making to move past him. 'Excuse me.'

'I followed you from Bank Top.'

'What were you doing up there?'

'Hoping to see you,' Bob said. His expression was open and sincere. She was so bloody naïve! She believed him! He could see it!

'Well, I wasn't hoping to see you.'

'You wanted a bit of fresh air?' he suggested sarcastic-
ally. 'Nice here, isn't it? The canal's the best bit.
Really fresh down there.'

Paula began to tremble. 'You were a thief,' she said,
more vehemently than she had intended. 'I'm not going
to pretend that you weren't.' She twisted her hands,
bending her fingers like plasticine. 'And the warden's
helmet, that was the worst thing!'

Bob lowered his head and looked suitably ashamed.
He could see she swallowed that too.

'But you saved my life,' she said, 'and I wanted to
thank you.'

That shocked him. Paula extended her woolly-
gloved hand awkwardly. Just as awkwardly, dislodged
suddenly from his play-acting, Bob took her hand.
Why did he suddenly feel nervous? The words that
usually came so glibly to his lips wouldn't come.

'Did I?' he stuttered.

'Of course you did.'

She disengaged her hand, smiled faintly and walked
away. Bob watched her go, unable to find his voice
until she was nearly lost in the gathering dark.

'Will you come for that drink?'

She stopped and turned, frowning. 'In a public
house?'

The Blue Anchor was crowded. A pall of grey and
yellow smoke hung above the chattering heads in the
public bar. Paula had never seen so many flat caps in
one place at one time, and she had certainly never seen
so many men keep their heads covered indoors. Bob

41

led her to a spot near the middle of the floor where the crowd was not so dense. He asked her what she would like, then left her stranded as he pushed his way through to the bar. The barmaid, Sue, who had the threads of a relationship with Bob, stared pointedly as she collected glasses. Jacko, his sparse hair pasted flat over his bald head, watched over the rim of a pint glass. Miss Thwaites, at her usual table with Mrs Thomas and Fred Spence, also assessed the woman: not Mafeking Park, but not far off it.

'She looks nice,' Mrs Thomas observed.

'Skin deep,' Miss Thwaites said. 'And she won't have much of that left when Sue gets hold of her.'

Sue did look ruffled. She glared as Bob swaggered to a gap at the bar. Dick Moxham came forward, put both hands flat on the bar and shook his head at Bob. He jerked his thumb at the NO CREDIT sign.

'I'll pay you tomorrow,' Bob said. 'I swear it, Dick.'

Dick moved aside and served another customer. The Americans, Joe and Earl, were shouting at Paula to come and join them. They augmented their powers of persuasion by waving their wallets and packets of Camel cigarettes. Paula began to look as if she might run for it.

Bob was meanwhile acknowledging an emergency. He looked at Jacko, who was standing near the bar; Bob's look signalled capitulation. Jacko made the merest nod. Bob made a move towards him and the deal was done. A glint of gold disappeared into Jacko's pocket, he nodded at Dick, and Dick smiled at Bob.

'Pink gin, please,' Bob said.

42

He hoped he had got that right, it was what she had asked for. Bob had never heard of it. Those within earshot, beer drinkers to a man, turned and looked. Dick was looking puzzled.

'You mean with Tizer?' he said.

'Aye . . .' Bob swallowed his ignorance and smiled. 'That'll be right. Aye. Gin and Tizer. Twice.'

The evening wore on and Bob made inroads. Paula began to talk about herself, and gradually the barrier between them diminished. The gin had something to do with that, though Bob believed he had worked a measure of his own magic. On his third trip to the bar he watched the American, Joe, show a girl some pictures from his wallet, which he appeared to keep in the side pocket of his jacket. Bob filed the observation, feeling that this was a night for taking note of every sign.

When he brought back two more gin-and-Tizers to the table Paula looked alarmed. 'I told you not to get any more!' She clapped her hands to her cheeks. 'Honestly, I only ever have sherry at Christmas.'

'That's all I ever have,' Bob said, straight-faced.

She stared at him, then burst out laughing. Their fingers touched as she picked up her drink. She withdrew her hand at once. She put the glass to her lips and took rather more than the sip she had intended.

'Better than pink gin,' she said. 'I couldn't think of anything else to say. Pink gin's what Mrs Winter drinks.' She made a face, a quick on-off. 'She'll have rung my mother. I'm trapped. That's why I came. This evening I felt that I knew everything that was going to happen to me for the rest of my life and that felt so horrible, so terrible that I didn't go home as I was supposed to, and I only meant to come a little way to see to ... Oh my goodness ...' She clapped her cheek again. 'What am I doing talking to you about this! Look at the time!'

The gin had flushed her cheeks. She had become animated and Bob was captivated by the transformation. Sipping her drink again, Paula saw the intensity in the way he looked at her, and she became flustered by that. She saw a woman going into the Ladies, got up rather clumsily and moved off in the same direction. Bob followed her with his gaze, which collided with a pair of unblinking eyes staring from the other bar. It was Mr Thrush, the rent collector. Bob tried to pretend he hadn't seen him. Sue, having seen Paula go, aimed herself at the table. Bob got up to go to the Gents but she stopped him.

'Why don't you just tell me you've got someone else?' she said.

'I haven't,' he said. 'Yet.' He winked, then, as her look turned a shade darker: 'No, no, listen, Sue –'

At that point Earl, very drunk, got up and tried to put an arm around Sue.

'Don't waste your time with him, honey,' he said. 'Come and help Earl win the war.'

Sue pushed the American away. It was not much of a push, but it was enough to overbalance Earl and he fell against Joe. There was a flurry, a small confusion with falling glasses. It lasted only a moment, but it was long enough for Bob to dip his fingers into Joe's jacket pocket and snatch the wallet.

When Paula came out of the Ladies she saw the commotion. She also saw Dick pushing Bob towards the door, assuming he was the cause of whatever trouble had arisen. Bob protested, but before he went back to get Paula he slipped into the other bar, stepped up to the rent collector and put a pound note in front of him on the bar.

'I knew I had it somewhere,' he smiled. 'Night, Mr Thrush.'

Bri was waiting in the shadows by the door as Bob came out. He stepped forward but slipped back again when he saw Paula. Bob was too engrossed to notice his little brother.

'What's wrong?' Paula asked.

Bob put on his concerned, I-did-it-all-for-you look. 'It can get a bit rough in there, sometimes,' he said.

He walked Paula back to the park, and they sat on a draughty bench at the top of the ornamental steps. There was a moon, and silvery mist clung to the steps. The setting would have been romantic, if it had not been so bloody cold.

'Why aren't you in the forces?' Paula asked him.

For a moment he thought she'd seen through him, but then he saw the innocence in her face. The glibness was still there when he wanted it.

'I'm still seventeen,' he said. 'I know I look older. Well, I tried to join up but my mother shopped me. I can't wait. The minute I'm eighteen I'll be there!'

'I wish I had your courage.'

'You can join up,' Bob said, leaning a fraction closer.

'I can't. She's fixed everything.'

'Unfix it.' He was consciously playing the wise adviser to impress her, but he also meant what he was saying. He wanted her to do something for herself. 'Go to the labour office in the morning. I'll see you there.' As she opened her mouth to protest he put up a hand. 'You've got to say you can do anything. Go on.'

'You can do anything,' she said.

'No, no. Daft bugger. *I* can do anything.'

'I can do anything.'

'That's the secret.' Didn't he really believe that? Well, in these moments he certainly did. 'That's magic,' he breathed. 'Oh, I'm going to do things!'

Paula was entranced. She watched the smooth sweep of his arm as it encompassed the world beyond Mafeking Park. Then he tried to kiss her. She jerked away from him and fumbled out her purse.

'Look,' she said, snapping it open, 'don't be offended. You bought all those drinks and I know you must have very little money.' She took out a half crown. 'Please take it. Please.'

Bob shook his head firmly. She pressed the coin into his hand. Seeing the discomfiture on his face, she folded his fingers round the coin and squeezed her hand, very briefly, around his.

'I must go,' she said awkwardly. 'Thank you for a very nice . . . for this evening.' She took a breath and looked at him squarely. 'I've never talked to anyone like this in my life before.'

'I never have,' Bob said, truthfully. And it *was* the truth! He *was* a hero! He'd saved her life. He was so overwhelmed by this that he was unprepared for her leaning forward sharply and kissing him with tightly closed lips. Just as swiftly she moved away from him and stood up.

'Have you never kissed anyone, either?' Bob said, rising.

She stared at him indignantly. 'Of course I have.'

'Magic lesson two. You have to shut your eyes and open your lips – didn't you know that?'

They kissed. For just a moment Bob tasted the warm, parting softness of her mouth and felt her hold him tight. Then she turned and ran off into the dark. He stood watching her go, his heart thumping.

'Tomorrow,' he called.

A punch hit the side of his head, knocking him across the path. Light flashed behind his eyes. He blinked as he crouched and brought up his fists. He saw the two men coming for him, Joe and Earl, separating as they closed in.

'You won't be going anywhere tomorrow, you bas-tard,' Earl snarled at him. 'Where's that wallet?'

Bob skipped back, evading the drunk man's clutches, and ran into a hammer blow from Joe. His ears sang. He staggered a couple of steps and sank to his knees. Three yards away young Bri was hopping up and down, ducking and weaving, being his big brother, willing him to fight back and win. He stopped jumping suddenly as Earl positioned himself and drew back his boot, ready to slam it into Bob's face. Bri and Bob had done this double act before: they were a team.

'Look out!' Bri screamed to Earl. 'Behind you!'

Earl glanced instinctively behind him and Bob grabbed his foot, jerking it back and upwards. Earl landed on his back, cracking his head on the top step. Bob scrambled to his feet. Earl got up a second behind him and both men went for Bob, arms spread, pincer-moving. Bob set his elbows at his sides and stiffened his neck. He stepped forward, dramatically narrowing the distance between them. He head-butted Earl square in the mouth and bent double, hitting Joe in the solar plexus. Both men reeled backwards, lost their footing and went clattering down the steps.

Bob tore off along the tree-lined avenue with Bri at his heels. As Bob ran he pulled the wallet from his pocket and threw it over his shoulder. Bri caught it and dived into the shrubbery beside the path.

Bob glanced behind him and saw the Americans, ghostly dark and silver in the moonlight at the far end of the avenue, starting to chase after him. He ran harder, his feet pounding the ground as he raced out through the park gates past the ARP post, over the bomb site, into the maze of even darker streets, through the ginnel where he knew every twist and turn and back alley, where they'd finally cornered Billy, his father – if he was his father – but they'd never corner him.

Behind his bush, Bri grinned as the Americans ran past, chasing the very article he held clasped sweaty-tight in his hand.

At half-past ten the next morning Paula came out of the Ministry of Labour office in Queen's Square and smiled broadly at Bob, who was waiting by the kerb. His right eye was puffed and coloured a rich regal purple. He took Paula's elbow and steered her through the frameworks of empty market stalls towards the central gardens.

'I've done it!' she said, beaming. 'She turned down Mrs Winter's application. It was so easy! Why was I so stupid?' She paused and frowned. 'What have you done with your eye?'

'Those two Yanks.' Bob shrugged with one shoulder. 'They were messing about with that girl in the pub. I had to sort it out.' He shrugged dismissively. 'What are you in?'

'I don't know yet. I asked for the WAAF. Oh, God . . .' Paula rolled her eyes. 'I don't know what I've gone and done, but I've done it!'

Spontaneously they turned to each other and hugged. When Bob tried to kiss her she turned her head away.

'Have you forgotten already?' he demanded. 'Magic lesson two?'

'Look . . .' Paula stepped back, rubbing her palms slowly against each other. 'I don't know what was in that gin and Tizer . . .' She paused, looked at him and shook her head. 'I wouldn't have done this but for you. I feel like a new person, a real person. But I can't see you again.'

Bob looked as if he had been slapped. He stared at her, waiting, seeing there was more.

'I've not been right honest with you. You see, I'm engaged.'

'And you think that's it, do you?'

She was shocked at the sudden ugliness of his face and the violence in his voice. His fists were clenched.

Bri suddenly appeared, running across the square, waving his arms at Bob. He slid to a halt in front of them, his arms still waving, indicating the direction he had come, the words spilling out of his mouth, running into one.

'They've been round again wi' Yanks they know you're in Seaforth who's she?'

Paula stared from Bri to Bob. He looked away. Always, whatever happened, he knew what to do, what to say. But again, with her, he was losing his tongue.

'Who's been round?'

'It's because of the fight,' Bob said, his glibness returning.

'What's because of it?'

'I put one of the Yanks in hospital. Practically ' He winked at Bri with his good eye. 'Didn't I?'

Bri nodded automatically and swiped his sleeve across his running nose. Bob tried to steer Paula away.

'Is he your brother?'

Embarrassed, Bob glanced at Bri then turned to Paula with a little laugh. 'He comes from a poor family down our street. Don't you?'

Bri nodded again, bewildered.

'I look after him sometimes,' Bob added.

He looked beyond Paula's shoulder across the square. A jeep had drawn up outside the Army Office. A Redcap got out. Earl was with him. They appeared to be arguing. Bob took Paula by the shoulders and looked into her eyes. When he spoke his lips scarcely moved, and it was difficult to say whether the words were more of a threat than a promise.

'I'll not forget you.'

The next moment he was gone, running off among the tall grey buildings, followed by Bri. Paula watched them go. As she turned to leave the gardens she saw the American soldier and the Redcap go into the Army Office. Was that to do with Bob? Well, it no longer concerned her. She had thanked him. She had told him she was engaged and, when she got her posting, she would soon be out of Seaforth.

Out of Seaforth! She hurried across the square, excited, warming herself with the thought of what had happened in the labour office. At last, she was taking charge of her life – thanks to him, to that adventure, she'd changed it more in the last twelve hours than in the nearly nineteen years before.

6

The notices around the bomb site gave clear warnings – DANGER: KEEP OUT. The area had long since been picked clean of shrapnel and everything else of monetary or archival value by the children of the area. No one came near any more. It was four hundred by three hundred square yards of rubble with a solitary wall left standing at its midst.

Bob walked sullenly along the road that bisected the wilderness. Bri was beside him. They had run most of the way here from Queen's Square and Bri was still puffing.

'Mother told them, didn't she?'

Bri nodded. 'She gave them your picture. That one in Bridlington.'

'Cow. All women are cows. Bitches.'

'What about her back there?'

'She's the biggest bitch of all.' Bob lifted a stone and hurled it savagely at the wall. A few fragments dislodged and tumbled into the debris.

'Yank were telling Redcap he couldn't find a tart in a brothel,' Bri said. 'He said it weren't the money, but the letters in the –'

Bob dropped the stone he was about to hurl and took his brother fiercely by the shoulders, holding him as he had held Paula, gazing fiercely into his eyes. Bri gulped.

'Are you with me?'

'Yeh,' Bri croaked.

'Till death?'

Bri nodded, wide-eyed. He would follow his brother even there.

Early next morning Bri led Sue across the wasteland, taking her hand from time to time as they negotiated hummocks of brick and miniature craters. Half-way across Bri pointed to a pile that looked like most of the others. As they approached it Bob crawled out and stood up, slapping dust from his knees. He was already showing the effects of sleeping rough. A moment later a scraggy-looking mongrel came out of the opening and stood by Bob, flicking its tail from side to side.

'Where did you find him?' Bri said, patting the animal, getting his face licked in return.

'Bastard found me.' The dog turned its head and nuzzled Bob. 'Get out of it!'

Bri ran off a short distance and called to the dog. It hesitated, tongue lolling, then ran after him. Bob turned to Sue. They looked at each other. Sue's eyes were hard, her small mouth set tight. In daylight her plucked eyebrows were nearly invisible.

'Well,' she said, 'I'm here.'

Bob sighed. From his pocket he took the crumpled, greasy scrap of newspaper Bri had rescued from their bedroom. He showed it to Sue, with its headline, 'The

Modest Hero', and the picture of Paula. He felt quite proud, even at that moment, even if she was a bitch.

'So?'

'She came over to the Blue to thank me,' Bob said, 'that's all.'

'For screwing her?'

'For saving her life.' Bob's eyes softened and his head tilted a fraction. 'I love you, Sue.'

'You don't!'

'No.' He grinned. 'But it's nice when I say it though, isn't it?'

'You bastard!'

Sue lashed out. Bob caught her hands, dropping to his knees and pulling her with him. Ten yards away Bri saw them go down together. He shrugged. They always seemed to be doing that. Boring. Bri unwrapped a much-chewed piece of gum from a scrap of paper and popped it in his mouth, chewing vigorously to soften it. Then he ran off across the piles of rubble, leaving them to it. He yelled at the dog to follow him, which it was doing anyway, and he tried out the name he had decided to give it: 'Come on then, boy, come on, Tiger!'

The daylight and the setting were a huge hindrance but Bob did his best. He kissed Sue on her high cheekbones and on her mouth, the soft pecking kisses she liked, and breathed warmly on her face as he moved to her ear and nibbled the pierced lobe. One arm was around her shoulder, drawing her close, while his free hand wandered up under her skirt. He stroked her slowly, expertly, rushing nothing, making a fresh reality among the ruins, making Sue gasp and tremble.

She sat up abruptly and pulled his hand out from under her skirt. Bob moved in close beside her, holding her again, passing his hand lightly over her hair.

'You're the best, Sue,' he said in a low voice. 'The only one. I mean that.'

He kissed her gently on the cheek, then on the mouth. She shuddered and touched his face. As he moved back she stared. His hand was right in front of her, and it was holding the stolen wallet.

'Will you find this in the pub?'

'I told them I saw you take it,' Sue said.

'You made a mistake.' He pressed his lips to her temple, warming the soft skin. 'I know I've been a bastard, Sue. A right bastard, but I am going to be different. I swear it.' He brought out the tattered clipping, held it up. 'That night was magic. I realized I could do anything, be somebody.'

His voice was so intense and sincere, that even in the light of so much bitter experience, Sue was still moved.

'I swore that night I'd never steal again . . .' he continued passionately.

The sound enchanted her, the timbre of his voice through his chest, the feel of his breath on her face. She was so hypnotized it took a few moments for the meaning of the words to reach her. When it did she leaned away from him.

'But you did,' she said, exasperated with him, with her. 'You stole that bloody wallet!'

Bob was looking at the wallet as if it had landed in

his hand from nowhere. He put it on the ground.

'It's . . . habit.' He spoke with genuine despair. She had known him long enough to recognize the difference – he *was* genuine somewhere. That was what was so exasperating – and so attractive. She burst out laughing. 'You do talk a load of crap,' she giggled. 'I don't know why I listen to you.'

Bob drew her close again and kissed her cheek. Sue looked down at the wallet. After a moment she picked it up and put it in her pocket.

A couple of days later Bri took two empty stout bottles to the off sales counter at the Blue Anchor. He looked about him furtively as Sue came forward. She smiled brightly at him.

'He says,' Bri whispered harshly, 'is it OK?'

Sue nodded. 'Where is he?'

'Dunno.' Bri said it with perfect aplomb, not even blinking.

Sue went to the cash register, rang up NO SALE and took out some coppers. She came back and put two pennies by the returned bottles. Then she held up two more pennies.

'What's her name, Bri?'

'Paula.' His face stiffened, as if he had said too much, then he added, 'He says she's the biggest bitch of all.'

She felt a sickness in her stomach, a surge of jealousy. She wouldn't mind being called the biggest bitch – that meant much more than all his meaningless rubbish about love.

Expressionless, she pushed the four pennies across

the counter and watched Bri snatch them up. 'Tell him I'll see him tonight,' she said. 'Usual place.'

Bri nodded and left. Sue turned, lifted the flap to the other bar, and went through. A Redcap was there, sitting back in his chair with a pint glass in his hand, his shiny boots and snowy gaiters propped on another chair. He smiled broadly at Sue, openly admiring her painted legs.

'Very nice,' he said, and drained the glass. He put it on the table and looked at Sue. 'Where exactly did you find the wallet?'

That night it was foggy again, cold, ground mist clinging to the bottoms of trees along the avenue through the park. At a few minutes past ten the silence was broken by the sound of footsteps and someone whistling 'How High the Moon'. After a minute the whistling stopped and so did the footsteps. Then the whistling started again; this time the tune was 'Lili Marlene'.

Sue, waiting near the foot of the steps, heard the whistling and responded with a snatch of 'Lili Marlene'. Bob came nearer, still whistling. Behind Sue two Redcaps were crouched, watching. One of them nudged Sue and grinned as they slipped into the cover of bushes by the side of the steps.

Bob appeared at the top of the steps, sauntering jauntily, a lit cigarette in his hand. He stopped, seeing Sue, and took a final drag on the cigarette, making the end a fuzzy bright glow in the mist. Sue began to shake. She caught the inside of her lower lip between her teeth and bit on it, with a little wince of pain. Bob flicked the cigarette away in a red arc and came down the steps, smiling. It was that smile that did it, that cheeky rotten smile that both cut her to the heart and made her curse herself as she screamed: 'Run, Bob! Run!'

Swearing, their timing gone, the Redcaps broke cover and charged after Bob as he leapt up the steps, taking them two at a time. He stumbled at the top, recovered and broke into a headlong run, hearing the boots clattering after him.

They chased him right through the park and out on to the road, which was visible only in the hazy masked headlamps of a car easing its way through the fog. By then one of the Redcaps had dropped back, but his partner was determined and when Bob hit the roadside he was close behind and gaining.

Running blind for most of the way, Bob made it to the bomb site and dodged through the piles of debris. The Redcap followed but began to lose ground, using his torch, getting confused by the shadows dancing in all directions from the heaps of rubble. He stopped to take air into his burning lungs, then clamped a hand over his mouth, making himself hold his breath as he listened, straining his ears. He hadn't been mistaken. Somewhere, not far from where he stood, Bob was standing too, motionless, catching his breath. The sound rasped across the air as clear as any signal. The Redcap turned his head, inch by inch, pinpointing the direction of the sound.

Bob was five yards away, standing a few feet back

from the edge of an enormous ditch rimmed with slippery mud. It was a spot where the foundations of a house had collapsed, leaving the cellar wide open to the sky. Bob's daylight memory of the ditch was clear: it was very deep, and there was no easy way round. He moved back a few feet more and hunched over, holding the image of the ditch in his head, getting ready to leap over it.

The Redcap heard Bob move and turned in his direction. He heard him move again and took off after him, certain of his course, heading straight for the target.

Bob heard him coming. He took a quick short run up to the lip of the ditch and threw himself forward in a flying leap. Cold air rushed past his face and watered his eyes as he sailed to the other side. He landed with a wet thump and felt himself slide backwards on the mire. He flailed with his hands and caught hold of a tangle of exposed plumbing pipes. He hung on to them with all his strength. Laboriously, hand over hand, he dragged himself up the slippery side and on to the hard ground at the top.

The Redcap saw the dark gap of the ditch as he approached it. He decided to make the jump without breaking stride. He simply quickened his pace and gathered himself forward, shifting his centre of gravity as he had been taught to do in obstacle training. He pounded towards the edge, breathing carefully, increasing his speed with every stride.

At the high lip of the ditch he threw himself forward, bending low to cut the wind resistance. His boot slipped on the edge as he took off, costing him half his thrust. He sailed forward then dipped sharply, landing with a series of bumps and splashes and settling in the rancid sewer water at the bottom.

Sue and the other Redcap came blundering across the rubble a couple of minutes later. Sue stopped and listened, hearing the injured man groaning. They went forward carefully and eventually found the ditch. With a lot of effort and cursing on the part of his colleague, the injured Redcap was pulled from the mud and filth and laid out on relatively dry rubble. He was only partly conscious, and blood flowed freely from a wound on the back of his head.

By that time, Bob was well clear of the bomb site.

Shortly before twenty past ten, the doorbell rang at Mrs Wickham's house in Moorland Road, Albany Gardens.

Mrs Wickham, tidying up the supper things in the kitchen, turned and stared. The door bell was never rung at that hour. This constituted an event.

Paula heard it and went to the bedroom door, opening it a fraction. She heard the front door open, then there was a murmur of voices. Paula went out on the landing. From below, with perfect clarity, she heard the unbelievable sound of Bob Longman's voice.

'I'm a friend of Paula's,' he said. 'We met at the Winters'.'

Paula stared, transfixed, from the top of the stairs. Over her mother's shoulder she saw Bob, his clothes wet, bedraggled, his face showing patchily white through a layer of dirt. He looked up and saw her.

'Hello, Paula,' he said brightly.

Mrs Wickham turned and looked at her daughter. Bob took the opportunity to step into the hall and close the door. Both women stared at him. He stared back for a moment, then from beneath the mask of mud and grime, he flashed his most engaging smile.

7

He apologized to Mrs Wickham for calling so late, and did so in an accent that put him firmly in the middle class. His appearance on her doorstep at such an hour was unforgivable, he knew, but the car had broken down and he had been trying to fix it, without success.

'I'm Mrs Winter's new driver,' he added, by way of explanation. 'Sorry I'm so filthy. I had to get underneath the car.'

The name of Mrs Winter galvanized Mrs Wickham. 'You'd better come in,' she said. 'Clean yourself up.'

She showed him where the bathroom was and pushed Paula ahead of her to the kitchen, telling her to put the kettle on.

Bob was ten minutes in the bathroom. When he emerged, treading softly down the carpeted stairs, his face and hands were clean, his coat was brushed and his hair was slicked back. In the hallway he picked up a china ornament from the shelf and turned it over, valuing it from habit. He was peering at the maker's mark when Paula emerged from the kitchen.

He started to say something but she pushed past him and opened the front door.

'Get out.'

There was a distant sound of an ambulance bell. Bob scowled, staring past Paula into the dark. The kitchen door opened again. Behind Mrs Wickham, on the table, he saw a tray ready with neatly cut sandwiches. Mrs Wickham frowned delicately.

'Aren't you staying for a cup of tea?'

'Thank you,' he beamed, putting down the ornament. 'This is very nice.'

'Paula, take Mister –'

'Call me Bob, Mrs Wickham.'

'Take the young man into the front room.'

Paula shut the front door and practically dragged Bob into the front room.

Bob stood looking around him at the polished furniture, the armchairs with their antimacassars, the framed pictures and shining brass plaques on the walls. It was many notches below the room he had broken into at the Winter house, but to Bob this was still something of a palace.

When Paula heard her mother rattling about in the kitchen she turned on Bob. 'What are you doing here?'

'I love you.

'Don't be stupid!'

Bob pushed his face close to hers. 'Don't call me stupid when I say I love you!'

He had grasped her by the shoulders again, his fingers digging so hard they hurt. For a moment Paula was scared. The door opened and she pulled away sharply, bumping into a table.

'I thought you might manage a sandwich after your exertions.' Mrs Wickham smiled fixedly as she put down the tray and sat beside him. 'Just a memory of meat paste, you have to use your imagination . . .'

'I'm quite good at that,' Bob said. 'You have to be good at it these days, don't you?'

'You have that.' Mrs Wickham was sizing him up, testing what she could perceive of him against her fixed notions about men. Her calculations were transparent: she was deciding she liked him, even trusted him. 'Funny,' she said, 'we were just thinking of seeing Mrs Winter —'

'Mother!'

'— about Paula's posting.'

Bob looked at Paula. 'Did you get the WAAF?'

'Aircraft factory,' Mrs Wickham said, mortified. 'That's what she got. A job in a factory.'

Her voice rang with disgust. Bob looked shocked. Paula looked humiliated. To hear her mother talk, anyone would think she had set out deliberately to get the job. She was about to put up a defence when Bob, behind Mrs Wickham's shoulder, gave her a huge wink. It stopped Paula in her tracks.

Bob moved back into Mrs Wickham's line of vision. 'Do you want me to have a word with Mrs Winter?' he asked sweetly.

'Could you?'

''Course. No problem.' He licked his lips delicately. 'Lovely sandwich.'

'That is kind of you . . .'

As Mrs Wickham turned to Paula, Bob gave her another wink, broad and outrageous. Paula couldn't help herself grinning.

'You see,' Mrs Wickham said to Paula, 'there's always a way – what is the matter with you?' She turned to Bob. 'One minute she's up, the next she's down.'

Bob nodded, showing strong sympathy, which made Paula bite her cheeks to keep from laughing out loud.

'I wish she had an ounce of your common sense.' Mrs Wickham glared at Paula. 'Pour him some tea, can't you?'

Paula obeyed meekly, still finding it hard not to laugh. Mrs Wickham glanced at the clock and announced she was going up. At the door she said good-night, and told Bob it had been nice meeting him.

'Very nice to meet you, Mrs Wickham, very nice indeed. Good-night.'

As soon as the door closed Paula crammed a cushion against her face to smother her laughter. She recovered slowly, slipping the cushion away, shaking her head at Bob.

'I've never met anyone like you in my *life*! How do you do it? She *believed* you! You're a scream, you really are. She's fallen for you.'

She began to laugh softly and Bob laughed with her. When she put a hand over his mouth Bob took her by the shoulders, softly this time, holding her, drawing her close. For a moment she responded, then pulled away. The bright easiness of manner had gone as quickly as it came. She picked up the plate of sandwiches and offered it to him. He stared at her sullenly, then at the sandwiches. He snatched two and began eating with the exuberance of a man without hope of another meal.

'Just finish them and go,' Paula said. She looked at

her hands for a moment, somewhere to put her gaze. 'I'll phone Mrs Winter in the morning.'

'Why?' he asked harshly. 'What's wrong with the factory?'

Paula looked surprised that anyone could ask such a question.

'Women get over two pounds a week there,' he said, swallowing a wodge of bread.

Paula was surprised in two ways: at the amount, and that he could, quite casually, think of the unthinkable – her working in a factory. She watched Bob pick up the last sandwich, then put it down again. She went to the door and drew it open.

'You'd better go.'

Bob stood up. The sudden, thundering noise of a heavy lorry going past made him jump. Paula saw the anxiety cross his face.

'I can't go,' he said. 'They're looking for me. The Redcaps.'

'Why?'

He shrugged, flapped his hands. 'There was an accident. On bomb site. Look ...' He took a half-decisive step to the door. 'I'll just go, it's all right. I don't want to involve you ...'

Wasn't he genuine then? Just as he had been, for a moment, with Sue? But didn't that somehow start to unravel, like one thread will unravel a garment, all that had happened since they had first met?

'Those pictures,' Paula said, still hoping it was not true. 'You stole those pictures. The silver frames. From the Winters. Didn't you?'

Bob nodded.

'I knew it. I knew it the night I came over to Mafeking Park. Oh, God ...' She drew her fingers through her hair. 'What's been happening to me?'

'You knew?'

'Of course I didn't *know*!' she snapped. 'What am I talking about? What's happening? Have you told me everything?'

'Yes.'

'Everything?' she insisted.

'Yes!' He turned so angrily on her that she was almost apologetic for doubting him. Then when he saw her face he felt so guilty for leading her on again – what was happening to him, he thought, let alone her? – that it all came out. 'Well. There's the wallet.'

Her mouth opened by itself. 'Wallet?'

'I took it from the Yanks in the pub. That's why they were after me.'

Paula sat down and covered her face with her hands. Bob got on his knees in front of her and touched her fingers, prising them gently from her face. She pushed him away and jumped to her feet.

'You don't want me to get involved?' she hissed, struggling to keep her voice down. 'I *am* involved, you stupid fool! The Winters were asking me about those photographs in the silver frames.'

The implications came to her in a string as she stood there twisting her hands. She began to look frightened.

'They'll think I was with you in the pub. People will think ...'

She clapped a hand over her mouth. There was movement overhead, the sound of bedsprings creaking. Bob waited until the house was silent, then he spoke. His voice was measured and controlled.

'Nobody will think anything if they don't find me.'

A few minutes later Mrs Wickham crept to the bedroom window and looked down at the street. Faintly in the dark she saw Paula at the gate with the young man. They were whispering their goodnights. As he walked away and Paula returned to the house, Mrs Wickham dropped the edge of the curtain and went back to bed.

After several more minutes, having stood at the foot of the stairs listening, making sure her mother had settled down for the night, Paula crept out of the back door and down the garden path, carrying blankets and a pillow. She stopped by the door to the Anderson shelter. Bob appeared from the gloom beside her. Together they prised open the corrugated iron door and slipped inside. Paula handed the bedding to Bob and lit the oil lamp.

'Go first thing,' she said. 'Before she wakes up.'

Bob looked round the drab rusted interior, seeing where the water leaked in. He put down the bedclothes, smelling the damp mattress. There was a muffled scratchy scuttling that could have been a rat.

'I don't think I shall be sleeping in,' he said.

'Promise!' Paula hissed.

He looked at her agonized face and seemed to be moved suddenly. In a gentle, contrite voice he said, 'I promise. I promise.' He kissed her.

'Don't, please don't . . .'

'I'm going away,' he whispered, staying close, stroking the side of her face.

An impulse seized her and she clung to him. 'Don't go away,' she breathed, letting him kiss her cheeks and eyes. 'Don't go away!'

'I've got to.'

'Yes,' she said, her breath catching as his hand covered her breast. 'Yes, you must, you must, we mustn't see each other again . . .' He drew her close and she moaned. 'Please don't. I'm afraid. I'm so afraid, God will punish us.'

'You don't believe in all that stuff, do you?'

'I believe in the punishment.' His hands had dropped behind her, closing on her buttocks and pulling her sharply against him. 'Don't!'

Frantically she resisted him and tried to twist away as he bent her backwards, kissing her neck, his body a hard insistent presence against hers. He spread his feet and she slipped, fell, clawing at him with one hand, trying to push herself up with the other. He came down quickly, enveloping her. They rolled over on the slats of the duckboard, Paula's foot hitting the side of the shelter.

'She'll hear us!' Paula moaned. 'She'll hear us!'

As she rolled on to her back Bob knelt up over her, readying himself. She watched in a fluttering panic and began kicking at him. He reached down and forced her legs apart. With a grunt he lowered himself sharply and entered her. Paula's eyes rolled back as the abrupt invasion convulsed her and made her gasp. Her foot shot out into the mud and water beside the board they lay on. The noise of it stilled her. Suddenly the most important thing was simply not to make a noise.

'Just be quiet,' she whispered. 'Just promise to be quiet . . .'

She went limp under him, submitting. He thrust himself at her, panting, his hips jerking faster and harder as he approached his climax. A change came over Paula. She gripped his arms and began to move with him. Bob's back stiffened, he threw up his head and cried out. Fear leapt back into Paula's face and she pushed her fist frantically into his mouth, moaning softly as the warmth surged in her.

Bob's body stopped moving. He gazed down at her, his face placid. Paula unclenched her fingers and stared at them in the lamplight as if they belonged to someone else. She looked at Bob, her features soft, relaxed. She reached out her hand and put her fingers under the dripping water. Gently she anointed his face, touching his forehead, his cheeks, his lips and his eyes.

8

On a bitter cold night towards Christmas they met by arrangement at the park gates, then walked together to the Blue Anchor. In the warmth of the public bar they sat at a corner table, motionless, looking at one another. The swirling hubbub of other people, merry and relentlessly noisy, went unheard.

'You're sure?' he said.

Paula nodded. She was only too sure she was pregnant. She would never have said a word about it without being triple sure, without being certain beyond the faintest shadow of doubt. Now that the fact was shared she had a sense of relief. They sat in silence, glad of the noise while Bob adjusted his view of life.

The bar had a distinctly festive spirit that night. The brewer had made a delivery during the afternoon so the place was packed. An unimaginative cluster of cheap, drooping Christmas decorations had been plastered up near Churchill's photograph by the door. At the bar a few members of the Seaforth Brass Band, among them Jacko on cornet and Fred Spence on beer glasses, were making a joyous hash of 'White Cliffs of Dover'. When Paula finally spoke again she had to manage the trick of raising her voice to make Bob hear, while keeping it low enough so no one else would.

'We could get married,' she said, making it as casual as she could.

He stared at her. 'You wouldn't marry me. Would you?'

She stared back, her eyes bright and candid. Of course she would.

'What do we live on?' he said.

'I get over two pounds a week at Winter's.'

'What do I do? I don't want to live in Mafeking Park for the rest of my life.'

'Well, neither do I. What else do you suggest?'

'Get rid of it.'

The remark was like a punch. Paula shoved back her chair and stood up. Bob took her by the arms, forcing her to sit again. She resisted him and people began to notice. When she realized they were staring she submitted and sat down again.

'I'll buy you a drink,' Bob said. 'Pink gin?'

He strode across to the bar, got half-way and came back. Paula took a ten-shilling note from her purse and gave it to him. He went to the bar and stood joking with Fred Spence while Dick got the drinks.

When he came back he put down the drinks and eyed Paula warily. 'I'm sorry,' he said, sitting down. 'It was the shock.' Her head was down, avoiding him, but he saw the glint of a tear track on her cheek. 'Here – what are you crying for?'

She sniffed as Fred and the improvised band at the bar struck up with 'How High the Moon'.

'I'm not crying,' she said, looking at him, blinking.

'You know how much I love you.'

'I don't.'

From asking what they were going to live on, he went from one extreme to another. 'I'm going to make a fortune,' he told her, 'and you're going to help me spend it.'

She looked incredibly vulnerable. Bob leaned close and kissed her with great tenderness. Her lips stayed tightly pressed together. He moved back a fraction and said, 'Magic lesson two.' Her lips parted and he kissed her again, reaching out to hold her as Jacko threw his heart into 'How High the Moon'.

Later Paula let herself into the house in darkness, closing the door quietly behind her.

'Is that you?' Mrs Wickham called from upstairs.

'Yes.' Paula put on the chain. She went to the foot of the stairs. 'Mother . . .'

The old bed creaked as Mrs Wickham turned over, settling. Paula sighed.

'They said it would all be over by Christmas,' she said, hearing a grunt from upstairs.

She sat down on the stairs, gazing at the faint light on the glass at the door. She was as motionless as her mother's china ornaments, her eyes bright in the dark. She called back a moment of sheer sweetness when the music had soared, when people sang and Bob held her, enclosing her with his tenderness. She pictured the moment, feeling its warmth, and tried to hold to it like sanctuary.

At 18 Kitchener Street Bob was staring out of the bedroom window at the terrace opposite, and beyond it to the factory by the canal. The hulking shadows and dull-shining slate roofs looked to him like the architecture of a prison. He felt trapped, robbed of choice. It was the worst thing in the world – to have no choice. She should have been more careful. And the stupid bitch wanted to keep it!

His feet began to feel the cold and he moved back from the window, shivering. He had taken off his boots but still had on his clothes. Keeping them on, he clambered into bed. Bri was lying diagonally, taking up most of the space. Bob shoved him and Bri punched out angrily, staying asleep, muttering as he moved over and made room.

Bob lay flat on his back and stared up at the crazed ceiling. Through the thin wall little Dora coughed, a fearsome rattle deep in her chest. Vera said something, soothing the child, who coughed again, then was quiet.

Bob went on staring at the cracks, listening to the coughs, the crying out of a child, the whispering rustle of a rat, an argument somewhere, perhaps in the ginnel, the night sounds of Mafeking Park. That was where they would have to live. Where else?

Next morning, early, Bri and Tiger went with Bob to Queen's Square. On the pavement outside the Army Recruiting Office they stopped and Bob said something to Bri, who nodded and looked at him with very serious eyes. As Bob walked away on his own Bri stared after him, absently stroking Tiger's ear.

In the Army Recruiting Office the Sergeant and a Redcap were pouring their first cup of tea of the day.

They had their heads together, deciphering an official memorandum, when the door opened and the bell sounded.

'Morning,' Bob said.

'Morning,' the soldiers muttered, looking up briefly.

They looked back at the document in front of them, then suddenly the Redcap's head jerked up. He stared, mouth open an inch, his eyes narrowing as Bob flashed him a cheery smile.

The Redcap came forward.

The edges of Bob's smile drooped a fraction and he threw a glance at the open door, but the Redcap was there already, shutting it. He bolted it, too, just to be sure, and turned to Bob again.

'Good morning,' he said briskly, as Bob clung gamely to the remains of his smile.

9

On a patch of ground by the foot of the park steps boys played football as Paula and Bri, standing nearby, conducted a small transaction. Paula held out a letter. Bri said something to her and she produced a coin. He took it, flipped it in the air the way his brother had shown him, caught it, then took the letter and ran off to join the other boys.

For a moment Paula stared beyond the gate to Mafeking Park, her eyes dreamy, taking in nothing until she noticed someone was marching smartly towards her. She turned quickly and made to climb the steps.

'Hey, you. Paula.'

She stopped and turned. Sue approached her and stopped a couple of feet away, smiling tightly, bitterly.

'I think we have something in common,' she said.

'I don't think so.' Paula did her best to sound cold and distant.

'Forget him.' Sue made a face. 'He deserves what the Army does to him in the glasshouse.'

'Glasshouse?'

'That's where they put deserters.'

'He wasn't a deserter!' Paula said indignantly.

Sue laughed. 'Why do you think they were after him?'

Paula was suddenly bewildered, her feelings adrift. She turned to go, then faced Sue again. 'Do you know where he is?'

'No.' Sue shook her head, and now she did not appear so aggressive. The hardness submerged as she deduced something from Paula's taut, desperate face. 'Are you . . .?' She nodded at her middle. 'You are, aren't you?' Sue shook her head. 'Do you want the address of the woman I used?'

Paula swallowed sharply, too shocked to respond. She did not miss the implication of *I used*.

'She's a chiropodist. Takes your corns out at the same time.'

'I . . .' Paula shuddered, her mouth twisting. 'I don't know what you're talking about.' She moved away quickly, half running.

'You stupid cow!' Sue shouted after her. 'You'll have to get rid of it!'

Paula kept moving, hiding her distress, pretending not to hear Sue's parting jibe.

'I wondered why he got caught by the Army so easy!'

At the house in Moorland Road Mrs Wickham was in Paula's bedroom, polishing the dressing-table. Halfway through the job she stopped, noticing something was missing. She went to the wardrobe, reached up and took a key from its hiding place. She opened the dressing-table drawer. A framed photograph of Richard lay inside. She looked at the spot on top of the dressing-table where the picture used to stand, trying to draw understanding from the state of affairs. She did not try for long. After a few seconds she shrugged and rummaged further into the drawer. She found a bundle of letters, a bottle of aspirins and a pair of knitting needles.

'That'll be the day when you knit, madam,' she murmured.

She heard the outside door open and shut the drawer quickly, locking it and putting the key back on the wardrobe.

Paula closed the door and stood in the hall, unbuttoning her coat. She could hardly remember getting there from the park. She felt like killing herself. The words hammered in her head. *Do you want the address of the woman I used?*

She glanced at the hall table and felt her heart jump at the sight of a letter there. She snatched it up then dropped it again, seeing the handwriting. She put down her snap tin and took off her coat, under which she wore a boilersuit.

Upstairs she found her mother vigorously polishing the dressing-table.

'Hello, love.' Mrs Wickham smiled brightly. 'See your letter from Richard?'

Paula nodded, turning back the bed sheets and pulling out her nightdress.

'What's happened to his photograph?'

Paula thought for a moment. 'Frame's broken.'

'You look peaky,' Mrs Wickham said.

'I've just come off night shift, haven't I? That woman –'

The words burst out of Paula before she could stop

them. She sat on the side of the bed, clutching her folded nightdress on her knees.

'What woman?'

Paula shook her head. 'Nothing. She ... She's on the same bench, she's not married, she got – up the spout, they call it. They really are revolting some of them. She got rid of it. Like having her corns out, she said.'

Mrs Wickham was scowling, her hands before her, one clasping the back of the other.

'How old is she?'

'About my age.'

'I hope her mother puts her on the streets! Where she belongs!'

Paula stared at her, her mouth dry. 'Is that what you would do?'

'I would!' Mrs Wickham said on the way to the door. 'I –' She paused and her face went rigid. 'You haven't been doing anything with Richard you shouldn't, have you?'

'With Richard?' Paula turned away, laughing, the very idea of Richard ... coming as a relief. 'For God's sake, mother ...'

Mrs Wickham sniffed and refolded her duster, heartened by Paula's response. 'You get into bed, love,' she said, going to the landing. 'I'll bring you a nice cup of tea.'

In a ruined French farmhouse, in what had once been the kitchen, a dented British Army helmet lay in the centre of the big kitchen table. Behind the table sat

Captain Warburton and beside him Second Lieutenant Gray. Bob Longman and Arthur Spence stood at attention facing the officers, with a stony-faced Sergeant McCulloch at their backs. All five men wore the uniform of the North Yorkshires.

Captain Warburton nodded at the helmet, which was Bob's, and which had been dented by a bullet from the rifle of a French farmer.

'About the nearest you've come to action, isn't it, Longman?'

'Yes, sir,' Bob replied smartly. 'Permission to speak, sir? The chickens we took were requisitioned.'

Second Lieutenant Gray looked intrigued, and not a little amused. 'Requisitioned?'

'Roast for the officers' mess, stew for the sergeants', sir.'

With an effort Gray kept his face straight. He was attuned to the fact that Bob's strategy, under questioning or on a charge, was to respond like a textbook soldier, and to take the procedure right up to the border of caricature. Gray found that very amusing. Captain Warburton, on the other hand, had no detectable sense of humour.

'Who requisitioned them?' Gray asked.

'Can't remember, sir,' Bob snapped.

Captain Warburton waved his hand as if he were swatting a fly. 'See if you can jog their memory, Sergeant.'

'Sir!' McCulloch barked. 'About turn! Quick – march!'

He marched them to the far side of the farm yard,

by the latrines at the perimeter of a broad field. Two other men were there: Bell, a fat and rather feckless youth who was known to everyone, inevitably, as Ding-Dong, and a raw-boned Scot just as predictably nicknamed Jock. McCulloch studied the men with theatrical disgust. He puffed his red cheeks as he ran his eyes from boots to berets, then he stood back and addressed them.

'I am Sergeant Mad McCulloch. You are the shit squad. You have had it easy. The Gerries are running so fast you think you will never catch up with them.' He cocked his head sharply. 'I have news for you. I am worse than the Germans. By the time I have finished with you, you'll be screaming to go to the front line.'

He stepped close to Bob and walked slowly round behind him. The malice in his eyes left no doubt about who would be the focus of this exercise.

'Name and last three.'

'Longman eight seven zero. Sergeant.'

McCulloch nodded. 'I know you,' he told Bob. 'You think you belong to yourself, but you do not. You belong to the Army. To me. Scrounger. Thief. Deserter.' He pointed to Arthur Spence, who was trying not to look nervous. 'Do a runner, Longman, and he has orders to shoot you, you mismade lump of shit.'

This was the area of human interaction where Bob had little control of himself. He did not take abuse well, and he took it least well from this kind of bastard. As McCulloch ranted at him Bob stiffened his back and warned himself not to slip, not to give him the satisfaction.

'Run!' McCulloch suddenly barked.

Bob gulped, unsure what to do.

'Go on! Run!'

Bob stared at the Sergeant. He saw bubbling saliva glint on McCulloch's lips as he pointed frenziedly to the far side of the field.

'*Run!*'

Bob started running.

'Double!' McCulloch yelled. 'Double!' He turned to Arthur. 'Prisoner escaping. Fire warning shots. Fire, you bastard, fire!'

Arthur froze with confusion and fear. McCulloch grabbed the rifle from him and fired. Bob dived into the hedge.

'I didn't say take cover!' McCulloch roared. 'I said run, you bastard! Double!'

McCulloch fired the rifle again. Bob scrambled out of the hedge with brambles tearing at his hands and face. He began running faster than he had ever run in his life. For ten minutes he charged round the perimeter of the field, and each time he slackened or stumbled McCulloch fired the rifle at him.

Finally, as the sixth bullet was being pushed into the chamber, Bob found he could call up no further resources. Nothing was left, his legs were heavy as lead and he could not run another inch. He sank to his knees, glaring at McCulloch with purest hatred. McCulloch appeared to take that with some satisfaction, as if it was the response he had been waiting for.

'Anybody else feel like running?' His voice was so quiet now, it sounded the voice of pure reason.

The others remained motionless. The only sound was Bob's ragged panting. With swift, practised movements McCulloch put on the safety catch and threw the rifle at Arthur.

'Account for five blanks, Spence. Reload with live rounds. In line, Longman. Move! Move! Dress from the left . . .'

IO

By ten o'clock McCulloch's shit squad was bedded down in the ruined barn that served as their billet. Torrential rain had fallen for hours and by now had found every opening in the shell-shattered roof. Water splashed and dribbled into buckets and mess tins. The men lay in half darkness at points between the water drips, on groundsheets for mattresses and kitbags for pillows, their boots lined up at their feet.

Tonight there was a treat: they were eating cake from a parcel Ding-Dong had been sent. In the circumstances their spirits were higher than they might have been, although Bob had found it difficult to get off the subject of his loathing for Sergeant McCulloch. Now, on his second chunk of cake, he decided to dismiss the topic with a statement of intent.

'I'll kill the bastard.'

'Where'd that get you?' Jock said. He chewed thoughtfully. 'Ah'd rather go to Liège. This tart . . . she was moaning for more, begging me to come back.'

'Mine was on her knees,' Bob said.

Jock held his hands out from his chest and cupped the air. 'She had knockers like pillows.'

Bob held his out even further. 'Like barrage balloons,' he said.

They both collapsed and began to simulate terminal ardour. Arthur was staring at them, his face deadly serious. Bob nodded for Jock to look at him.

'He was last in the queue when the truck came,' Bob said. 'Weren't you? He's never had it.'

''Course I've had it,' Arthur retorted. After a pause he added, 'Not recently.' The others laughed and he admitted: 'Never. I've never had it.'

There was more raucous laughter, but Arthur continued to look serious.

'That's the one thing I'm afraid of,' he said. 'Not dying – well, of course I am, but ... what I'm really afraid of is dying without having it.'

The laughter faded to nothing. For nearly a minute dripping water was the only sound. An instinct of charity, which he shortly afterwards regretted, made Ding-Dong give Arthur the last piece of cake. Jock, seeing there was no more to eat, lit a roll-up. They lay back, sated and thoughtful.

'What's it like?' Arthur said, throwing the question to whoever cared to answer.

'It's like ...' Jock's eyebrows rose as he inhaled. 'You know ...' He blew out smoke and watched it rise. 'A good shit, only better.'

'It's like double-cream ice-cream,' Ding-Dong said, 'smooth and slippery. It's like what I imagine – I've never had one – bananas taste like.'

'It's like music,' Bob said.

Arthur grinned, sensing one of Bob's send-ups, but the grin faded as Bob bent closer to him, his face as serious as his voice.

'Like an Indian snake charmer,' he said, 'hypnotizing the snake. Keeping it up. That's the trick. Up and up and suddenly . . . the world explodes! A miracle! Stars! And then . . .' He looked into Arthur's eyes. 'You have to perform the last trick.'

Arthur waited, frowning with concentration, mouth half open.

'Bugger off quick.'

Jock and Ding-Dong roared with laughter, then Jock waved an accusing finger at Bob.

'You couldn't get it up,' he said. 'Your tart told mine.'

'Sod off.'

Arthur caught the violent look on Bob's face, but Jock pressed on.

'She said –'

Bob swiped out at him, knocking the cigarette from his hand. 'She had a dose!' he snapped. 'I wasn't going to dip my wick in that! Now shut it!'

Later, when the other three were asleep, Bob lay listening to the pounding rain and the wind. He stared at the dribble of water running into the bucket near his head, trapping the light in a quivering line of dull silver. He looked at it and remembered Paula, reaching out her hand and catching the water, touching it to his face.

He had remembered her that night in Liège, too, with the whore spread out under him, bucking her hips, exciting one minute, repulsive the next as an image of Paula invaded his head. The vividness stunned him. All desire for the perfumed little Belgian had vanished. He had shouted at her she was no good. He wasn't going to pay her, not for that. Then he had paid her, just to shut up, and let him get away.

It was frightening. He hadn't been able to do anything. Worse. He couldn't get Paula out of his head. That face. That look. Over and over again he went over that last meeting at the Blue, then lying in bed at Mafeking Park, the noises, like the noises of the rain drumming in his head now, then – a solution to everything – the Army!

Some bloody solution.

Why had he done something so appallingly stupid? Why, why, why?

He sat bolt upright, breathing hard, jumped to his feet and started kicking all the buckets around him. Water splashed over Ding-Dong, a mess tin hit Arthur and a bucket rapped Jock's elbow. They roared and swore at Bob as he kicked away the last bucket and sat on a school bench, covering his ears with his hands as the drips became loud slaps on the matting and the stone floor. With eyes clenched shut he began rocking back and forward as if he were in pain. The others stopped swearing at him and stared.

Gradually he became motionless and simply sat there, head bowed, his hands dangling between his knees. Arthur, Ding-Dong and Jock re-set the buckets, righted the mess tins, rearranged their bedding and eventually went back to sleep.

The rain stopped just before dawn. As light began to creep along the horizon, Bob finished tying his bootlaces and stood in the middle of the barn taking silent stock. He was fully dressed and his kit was in his pack. He bent to shake Jock's shoulder, then changed his mind. He crept quietly out of the barn.

The feel and smell of washed morning air brightened him. He gazed for a moment at the light where it was dawning, then moved off quickly, walking with care, heading for the far side of the courtyard where an archway led out on to the road. When he was level with the first of the company transport trucks he slowed down, then stopped, watching the sentry by the barn to make sure he was sound asleep.

Silently he opened the truck door, rolled on to the driving seat and pulled himself up behind the wheel. He went motionless then, glancing at the sentry and seeing a packet of cigarettes lying on his knee. It was a tantalizing sight, as good as a gift.

He opened the truck door again, slipped out and crossed the courtyard on his toes. He crept up beside the sleeping soldier and reached out for the cigarettes. The sentry gave a sharp, shuddering sigh. His fingers opened reflexively and the rifle began to slip. Bob caught it just before it fell. The sentry's eyelids quivered. Bob slid the rifle gently back into the encircling fingers and held his breath. The sentry made a small contented sigh as he sank into sleep again. Bob took the cigarettes.

He made his way carefully back to the truck. He got to the door, grasped the handle and froze. Through the archway he saw a German soldier crossing into the courtyard at the double. Bob could hardly believe his eyes. He blinked, and as he stood there a second German soldier ran in, dropped to one knee and raised his rifle to a firing position.

As the gunfire started Bob threw himself to the ground. He looked out from under the truck and saw the sentry's forehead vanish in an eruption of blood and snowy flecks of bone. Incredibly he stood up, eyeless and screaming, until more bullets struck him and he fell.

Bob pressed himself close to the ground, pushing his face into the dirt and trying to hug it. Over his head a German machine-gun opened up. The stream of bullets tore into the side of the barn by the archway and blew in its windows. Through the noise McCulloch's voice roared, ordering the panicking soldiers to keep their heads down.

In all the farm buildings soldiers were crawling on floors, getting their kit together, looking for rifles. Then in the midst of the panic there was abrupt silence. The shooting had stopped. In the barn nearest the archway Sergeant McCulloch hooked his braces over his shoulders and raised his head cautiously to peer over the ledge of a window frame. A young soldier crept alongside him and looked outside. He could see the courtyard, the vehicles, the dead sentry. There was no sign of movement, except for a bird flying from tree to tree. The soldier stood up. A volley of machine-gun fire hit him in the chest and threw him against the far wall. Another soldier, terrified, began to scream.

'Get me the sodding Bren!' McCulloch shouted. 'Double! Double!'

The soldier went on screaming. Another one panicked, stood up and took three bullets in the face.

'The bloody *Bren*!' McCulloch roared.

Outside Bob raised his head an inch, looking for cover. He saw the dead sentry, lying a few yards away. His head looked like a bizarre blob of pink and crimson clay, jammed on the shoulders of his twisted body. Bob dropped down again as another burst of gunfire passed above him.

Lieutenant Gray ran into McCulloch's barn, bleary-eyed, hair awry. Captain Warburton was close behind him.

'Sergeant McCulloch!' Gray shouted. 'I need half your men!'

'Yes, sir! Rogers, Owen, Griffiths! Over here!'

The men clustered around Gray. Captain Warburton took charge of the remainder, directing them to positions at the windows. 'Spence,' he shouted, 'You take the Bren. Give covering fire.'

Gray urged his men forward. They ran out into the courtyard at a crouch, moving under the hail of covering fire from the windows. They spread out and ran for the shelter of the transport vehicles and sundry piles of rubble. As they scattered there was a burst of machine-gun fire and one soldier was hit. Another, dithering in the doorway of the barn, took a bullet in the arm and dropped to his knees, roaring with pain.

Bob lay for a second watching the chaos, seeing puffs and eruptions of dirt all around him as bullets strafed the yard. In a sudden panic he rose, dashed forward and rolled behind the cover of an upturned cart. He thudded to a stop against the elbow of Jock, who scarcely noticed him.

The firing stopped and again there was a terrible silence over the courtyard. Smoke curled and drifted across the emptiness. Men ducked down, hardly breathing, finding the stillness as hard to take as the gunfire. The only sound was the frightened whimpering of the soldier wounded in the arm.

McCulloch's head came up over his window ledge again. He could see German soldiers crawling behind the distant ammunition trucks. Whispering harshly, he ordered Ding-Dong and Arthur to follow him with the Bren gun. Together they ran up the stairs to the upper floor of the barn. They set up the Bren by the central window. From there they could see the source of all the damaging fire – five German soldiers manning a machine-gun emplacement behind an ammunition truck.

'Hold your Saturday night fingers,' McCulloch said, getting his eye to the sight of the Bren. 'Firing a rifle is all foreplay, remember. Imagine you have it up there. Gently, gently . . .'

Arthur, who had never had it up there, had the butt of his rifle against his cheek, his whole body trembling, his finger half an inch off the trigger in case he fired too soon. He glanced fearfully at McCulloch, who was hunched over the Bren, his face rigid with the intensity of the moment. As he took aim his lips drew back over his teeth and stayed there. His eyes narrowed behind his glasses.

'Fire!'

The German soldiers at the machine-gun were hit simultaneously by the fire of the Bren and two rifles. They died at once. McCulloch kept on firing as Germans scattered about the courtyard, breaking cover, trying to escape. Bodies dropped one after the other, falling headlong as they ran, colliding, slamming against walls with the impact of the bullets.

McCulloch finally stopped firing.

The smoke rose in slow thick skeins, revealing the carnage. Captain Warburton and Lieutenant Gray were staring up at the barn window. Bob and Jack did the same, seeing the wan, pale faces of their mates flanking the red-faced McCulloch. Soldiers began to rise slowly, looking around to see who was wounded. One man got to his knees, then cautiously stood up. Two more ran forward to the centre of the courtyard, grinning.

Noise punched the air again as a second German machine-gun opened up. The two soldiers went down, the second one's face and shoulder disintegrating as he fell. Men flattened on the ground again. McCulloch, stiff with rage, began firing at random, spraying the courtyard and the bodies of dead Germans as he tried to locate and obliterate his invisible target.

A truck was burning. Black smoke billowed low across the courtyard as Lieutenant Gray shouted orders to soldiers he could scarcely see. The cries of the wounded cut across his voice and were drowned, in their turn, by bursts of gunfire.

Bob and Jock were huddled like lovers. Bob's eyes were darting, looking for an advantage, an alternative. A light gust of wind made a clearing in the smoke and immediately he saw a possibility. He nudged Jock and pointed to the nearest truck, fifty or sixty feet away. Its nose was pointed out towards the open road, away from the Germans.

'Run on three,' Bob said, rising to a crouch.

'We'll not make it,' Jock protested, but nevertheless he crouched beside Bob.

'One, two . . . *three!*'

They darted across the courtyard, bent low, Jock stumbling and being pulled by Bob.

McCulloch saw them from his vantage point high in the barn. He started to yell at them but had to drop below the window ledge as machine-gun bullets tore into the frame. Splinters flew and brick shattered as he pressed himself to the wall beneath the window. Arthur and Ding-Dong were crouched there already, watching bemused as bullets raked a pattern of holes in the far wall.

Bob and Jock got to the truck and slammed themselves against the side. Jock struggled with the door handle, finally tore the door open and jumped in. Bob leapt in behind him. Jock fumbled at the controls for a panicky moment, then thumbed the ignition button. The engine started, coughed and died. It did it again. Panic began to derange Jock's eyes.

Across the courtyard McCulloch was running down the barn steps two at a time, carrying the Bren at shoulder level. The truck's engine fired as he ran out of the barn. He could see Jock wrestling with the unfamiliar gearbox. Bob grabbed Jock's arm and pointed at McCulloch, running towards them through the smoke and gunfire, yelling and waving his arms.

Jock grated the gears into reverse. McCulloch stopped in front of the truck and pointed the Bren. Jock slammed his foot on the accelerator and the truck shot backwards.

'Bastards!'

McCulloch fired from the hip, spraying bullets wildly into the truck. Jock craned his neck and clung tightly to the wheel, trying to weave a way out of the courtyard.

Suddenly everything shifted violently. For a moment of blind incomprehension Bob and Jock stared at each other as the ground under the rear wheels collapsed and the truck sank backwards into the hole, upending itself in the central refuse pit.

McCulloch fired again and Bob turned to see Jock take a direct hit on the forehead. The sound was like a rubber ball hitting brick. Jock's forehead split and blood sprayed the cabin. Bob screamed and dived low in his seat. He put his hands to his face and felt stinging. A moment later he saw blood drip on to his knee and felt a deep open groove on his cheek. Glass was splintered round him, crunching on the floor, stabbed into the seat.

There was sudden agitation at the side of the truck, rattling and shaking and banging. Bob looked up, glancing at Jock, seeing his dead face and the grey-pink gouts of brain on the splintered bone of his skull. The banging got harder and suddenly McCulloch jerked open the door. He looked crazy.

'You run towards the enemy, not away from them!' he screamed at Bob. 'Turd! Coward!'

McCulloch dropped the Bren gun and pulled Bob out of the truck. He was dazed and off-balance. He landed, staggered and found his feet, then McCulloch head-butted him. Bob slumped forward. He had no control of his arms or legs and the pain in his head was swelling, threatening to explode.

'Get up, coward! Up, you shit, or I'll kill you!'

McCulloch pushed and Bob staggered forward, half blind, unaware that he was moving towards the enemy. Bullets started to whine around his head. Panic shoved him on to a higher plane of consciousness. He reeled away from McCulloch, losing sight of him in the smoke, then seeing him again as he followed, pushing, punching. Bullets pocked up the ground around their feet as the Germans fired blindly through the smoke.

The rising level of danger became suddenly clear to Bob. He began fighting back, grappling with McCulloch, pulling him to the ground and rolling with him, trying to get behind the cover of a mound of rubble. He made it, catching a punch in the mouth on the way, managing to land a chop on McCulloch's neck as they moved behind the pile of bricks and slats and stones.

McCulloch's aggression eased as he realized how near they were to the enemy. He pressed his hands into the rubble and levered himself up, trying to get a bearing on the Germans and simultaneously locate an escape route. As he did that a German soldier threw a grenade directly at the mound of rubble.

The grenade took a clean line of flight and landed between Bob and Sergeant McCulloch. The younger man's reaction was more instinctive, more immediate.

If he'd had McCulloch's experience he would never have been so stupid. He got up to a crouch and watched the grenade roll towards his hand. It seemed very large, he could see the deep-scored divisions on its surface, the trigger-like grip, the depression where the pin had been. His hand appeared to reach for it incredibly slowly. He saw McCulloch staring, stiff, motionless.

Bob picked up the grenade, feeling its warmth as his fingers closed around the hardness. It felt as if it was sticking to his hand. He heard himself grunt as he drew back his arm. Everything seemed so *slow*. He saw the sky beyond the smoke, smelt cordite and cattle and a loamy richness that filled his nostrils. He rose and drove his arm forward, concentrating so much that he was barely aware they were firing at him.

The grenade left his hand and was airborne again. It was not a particularly good throw but it was long and the grenade travelled back in the direction it had come. As Bob sank down behind the rubble the grenade landed in the back of a truck behind which the Germans were taking cover. It rolled and came to rest against stacked ammunition cases. A German soldier saw the grenade and got half-way to his feet, his mouth open to issue a warning.

The grenade exploded. An instant later so did the entire truck. Bob pressed himself flat on the ground, his mouth in the earth as heat erupted from the sky, as buildings blew apart with a deafening, maddening roar. He was yelling and crying and clawing the earth. 'Paula Paula Paula Paula Paula Paula . . .'

At the far end of chaos and terror, coldness touched

his skin. A breeze. His eyes cleared. He saw Second Lieutenant Gray, Arthur Spence, Sergeant McCulloch, all walking on the torn earth, looking like ghosts. He was shaking and something hard was at his back. He moved his fingers and realized he was sprawled against a wall. There was only dull heaviness in his ears and a singing that wasn't really sound, it was more a feeling. He took in no sound at all. He was deaf.

He couldn't stop shaking and he was spitting earth from his mouth and dislodging it with his tongue from his teeth. He felt warmth where he sat and realized he was sitting in his own shit.

Time passed. His mind drifted, hearing his voice calling Paula's name over and over, hearing an explosion and feeling dry heat on the air that made his skin feel scorched. Then suddenly he was awake and being lifted to his feet, and he could hear, although his ears still rang. A rifle was being put in his hands and he was lining up with the others, who all had rifles and were pointing them at the other side of the yard where smoke still billowed. He brought his rifle up, aiming it, and realized he was obeying orders, although he had no idea how he was managing to do that.

They seemed to stand there for ever. Then, through the smoke, a German officer appeared. He was young, a haughty-looking man, broad-faced, confident. He wore a Red Cross armband and carried a white scarf.

He stopped, seeing the line of rifles pointed at him. Remaining calm, he saluted. Captain Warburton returned the salute and stepped forward. The rifles stayed levelled at the German.

'Captain Karl von Berner,' he said. 'I would like your permission to recover my wounded.'

Warburton nodded. He stared pointedly at the bodies of German soldiers scattered across the courtyard, then looked at Captain von Berner.

'Why don't you call it a day?'

Von Berner frowned delicately. 'I beg your pardon?'

'The war is over.'

The German stiffened. He raised a hand, indicating the sounds of tank and artillery fire in the distance. 'The war is far from over.'

Bob stared at Captain von Berner and for an instant their eyes met. Nothing made sense. It made no sense that he had left Paula. No sense that he was here. And what sense was there that such civilized behaviour, such *politeness*, existed at the heart of brutal carnage?

'Pick up your wounded,' Captain Warburton said.

II

The following day Second Lieutenant Gray and Captain Warburton inspected the crashed truck. Gray was openly shocked at the number and distribution of bullet-holes in the vehicle.

'Now I know why he's called "mad".'

'It's a good job he is,' Warburton said drily.

'He could have fired at the tyres,' Gray pointed out. 'He shot that man without warning!'

'They were deserting, Tony, for God's sake.'

They turned and watched as a vehicle approached.

'There's got to be an inquiry,' Gray said stubbornly.

The vehicle stopped some distance away. The door swung open and Lieutenant-Colonel Plummer, an athletic-looking man in his late thirties, got out and stretched his legs. His aide led him into the ruined farmhouse. Warburton and Gray began moving in that direction.

Warburton nodded at Jock's tarpaulin-wrapped body as they walked past it. 'What the hell good would an inquiry do? Particularly for him? Do you want his NOK to be told he was shot for desertion? Or died honourably, in action?'

'McCulloch will kill again,' Gray said stiffly.

'Then let's hope they're all Gerries. Or Longman.'

Lieutenant-Colonel Plummer had come to do one of the jobs for which he was principally engaged, which was to inject good morale where it was needed, and to sustain it where it had already been established. He was not especially good at that aspect of his work, which called for subtlety and a lightness of touch. Plummer was a man of clumsy wit, devoid of a real sense of humour but habituated, nevertheless, to using jokes and sporty metaphors at every opportunity.

In the farmhouse he addressed the assembled company, with Captain Warburton, Lieutenant Gray, Sergeant McCulloch and Bob Longman standing in a line at the front.

'At ease. I am sorry you weren't told there was going to be a show yesterday. I wasn't aware of it myself.'

There was an exchange of uneasy grins. Plummer leaned forward sharply, putting feeling into his voice.

'It was vital to hold this corner for the tanks to get through and you fought with great bravery. I feel as keenly as you do for the loss of colleagues and friends.' He paused. 'Sergeant McCulloch, your action has been noted . . .'

There was a small shifting of feet and a frown from McCulloch as he wondered exactly what had been noted.

'You valiantly destroyed an enemy section with . . .'

'Private Longman, sir,' Warburton said.

Plummer nodded and smiled awkwardly at Bob. 'Good throw from the boundary, I gather.'

Bob suddenly found himself emerging – at the double

– from shock. He recognized his situation at once – this was chameleon territory, where his native charm and his grasp of the moment could cut him a perfect slot. He smiled shyly.

'Bloody good job their stumper dropped it, sir.'

Spontaneous laughter. The air seemed to lighten as Plummer's awkwardness was defused.

'Good man!' He slapped Bob on the shoulder. 'Good man!'

Later that night Bob sat apart at one end of the draughty barn, drinking alone as Arthur and a few of the others played pontoon. The game, for Arthur, came to an abrupt end as he twisted on eighteen and went bust with a six. He threw down his hand and wandered unsteadily across the barn to where Bob sat holding a pencil, staring at papers spread out over his kit-bag. He was engrossed and didn't notice Arthur until he stepped up close and saluted.

'Robert Longman. VC and bar. Sir!' Arthur grinned.

Bob whipped the papers off the kit-bag and folded them.

'What are you doing?' Arthur asked.

'Nothing.'

Arthur caught the tightness on Bob's face as he tucked the papers into the bag. 'What's up?' he insisted, curiously.

'Nothing,' Bob snapped, turning away. 'Look, bugger off, will you?'

In another barn across the courtyard, Lieutenant Gray sat drinking from a mug of tea and writing a letter to his mother. When he had completed the first couple of lines he turned up the wick of the lamp and read them.

'Dear Mother ... Not a great deal to tell you, except I am well and ...' He glanced around at the bullet-holes in the walls and the piles of fallen plaster, then added, 'am sitting in this beautiful village somewhere in ...'

He looked up again and saw Bob standing in the doorway.

'Permission to speak, sir.' As an afterthought he saluted.

Gray looked at him with distaste. 'You're drunk, man.'

'I couldn't say what I want to say if I were sober, sir.'

'Is it about Sergeant McCulloch?'

'Sergeant McCulloch?' Bob frowned for a moment. 'No, sir, I don't think so.'

'You don't think so.'

'It's about a girl, sir.'

Bob came forward and stood in front of the table. He brought out a letter Paula had sent. He handed it to the Lieutenant, and explained briefly, awkwardly, that Paula was expecting his baby.

Gray glanced at the two much-folded sheets of paper. 'You're sure it's yours, are you?'

'Oh yes, sir. She was a virgin. And ... I think it was that first time. You know. You know when you know, like ...'

Gray looked at him. 'The only knowing is in the biblical sense.'

'Beg your pardon, sir?'

'Well you can't really *know*, can you?'

'Oh yes, sir. I always know.'

'This has happened to you before, has it?'

'Not like this.'

'What do you mean?'

For once, Bob ran out of words. He simply grinned and stood cracking his fingers.

'Look,' Gray said, pointing to a chair, 'for God's sake sit down.'

As Bob sat Gray stood up. He read the letter, then looked at Bob. 'You love her? Is that what you mean?'

Bob laughed.

'There's no need to be embarrassed. It does happen. Even to people like you.' He paused, looked at the floor. 'I'm sorry, I shouldn't have said that. She seems to be in love with you.'

'Does she?'

'You've read it,' Gray said, 'numerous times, by the look of it.'

He handed the letter back to Bob, who sat staring at it.

'First and only love,' Gray said, quoting. 'For ever and ever, etcetera – I shouldn't think you could get much clearer than that, do you?'

Bob shook his head dumbly.

'She writes quite well, in fact,' Gray said. 'Her powers of expression haven't suffered from too much education.'

That appeared to sail over Bob's head.

'Good-looking, is she?'

Bob nodded. He tapped the letter on his knuckles for a moment, then looked up at Gray. 'I nearly did a runner yesterday morning, sir. I felt I had to see her to tell her . . . to tell her . . .' He shrugged.

'That was stupid,' Gray told him. 'Stupid.'

'Yes, sir.'

'What would you have done?'

'I don't know, sir.' He looked Gray straight in the eyes, all his cockiness and his other defences gone. He still held the letter. Gray was at something of a loss.

'You've told her how you feel?'

'I left afore – I didn't realize . . .' Talking about it suddenly released the pain. He realized what he had done. Gray was right. He *was* in love with her. And he had left her. He couldn't imagine ever being in love with anyone else and he had thrown it away. The words came out, sharp and jagged. 'It's driving me mad, sir, thinking of her, thinking of what I've done.'

'But . . .' Gray frowned. 'You've written to her?'

Bob stared at the letter blindly. 'I can't write, sir.'

Gray stared at him. Now Bob had said it, a little of his confidence appeared to come back. He watched the Lieutenant sit down and gazed candidly at him.

'Could you write to her, sir?'

Paula turned on the taps and emerged from the bathroom as her mother came up the stairs carrying a tin of Eno's Fruit Salts and a glass of water.

'What are you doing?' Mrs Wickham demanded.

'Making pancakes. What's it look like? I thought you were in bed.'

Mrs Wickham patted the front of her dressing-gown. 'I don't know what were in that corned beef.' She shook her head. 'You've already had a bath this week. How can Britain save coal when –'

Paula swept past her and went downstairs to the front room. There was one shelf of books. She took down a thick red one, *The Family Health Guide*, and made to leave with it. At the door she stopped. Her mother hadn't gone into her room, she was in the bathroom turning off the taps. Beyond the point of caring, Paula opened the book to a page she already knew. She gripped it by the edge and with a sharp series of jerks tore it out. She folded it, stuck it in her dressing-gown pocket and put the book back on the shelf.

By the time she got upstairs again her mother had gone back into her bedroom, but she still hadn't settled down. Indigestion could keep her on the move for hours. Paula went to her own room and pushed the door almost shut. The curtains were not properly closed and through the gap she could dimly see the air raid shelter. She stared down at it for a minute, then closed the curtains.

At the dressing-table she took the key from its hiding place and opened the drawer. She removed a knitting needle, put it in her dressing-gown pocket, then went and sat on the bed. For a few minutes she looked at the page she had torn from the book. It had a short column about the womb, and alongside it a drawing. She did her best to memorize the drawing.

She finally put the page back in her pocket and took

a pad of Basildon Bond from the drawer. She flipped it open, seeing snatches of a letter she had written.

'I never expected to feel anything stronger than the love I felt for you, but the hatred is stronger . . .' And on the second page: 'Old wives' tales . . . I've tried gin, jumping off the table, it's as tough as you . . .'

She tore the pages out and took them into the bathroom with her. For ten minutes she sat in the hot bath, trying not to think, letting the warmth numb her. When the water began to cool she climbed out and towelled herself. She took the letter from her pocket, read it through, then tore it into small pieces and dropped them into the lavatory. From her dressing-gown she took out the knitting needle. Her hands shook and she noticed her mouth had turned very dry.

She squatted, putting her back against the side of the bath. For a moment her fingers trembled so badly she could not control them. She took a deep breath and braced herself. She held the needle with both hands and inserted the tip gently, holding the picture in her head, seeing the angle of the canal, the position of the cervix. The needle moved freely. She steadied it, closed her eyes, imagining the angle of the point, then pushed it sharply inward.

The pain was unbelievable. Her throat locked and for a whole minute she could only gasp, standing on her toes with her hands flattened against the wall.

The spasm passed. She pulled out the needle and dropped it in the washbasin. There was blood on her hands. She rinsed them, turned to the mirror and had to wipe away the steam to see her face. She looked grey. Something moved low in her abdomen and she winced, feeling sick. She made it to the lavatory bowl and sat there, feeling herself fade as the terrible loosening increased, making her feel she had begun to unravel.

The next thing she noticed with clarity was the noise. She sat upright, staring. The handle of the bathroom door rattled.

'For God's sake, Paula!' Mrs Wickham called. 'You're in there morning noon and night!'

'Minute,' Paula said, forcing her voice to be light, getting up and tugging the lavatory chain without looking down. It gurgled but did not flush. She jerked it again, feeling dizzy, noticing how white her hands and arms had become. This time the toilet flushed. She grabbed her dressing-gown and put it on. There was blood on the front. She undid the sash and re-folded it so the stain was hidden. Her hands were clumsy as she worked at tying the sash. It was as if the fingers were not hers.

'Paula! I'm desperate!'

Paula swallowed hard, trying to think of something to say. She had to hold on to the wall suddenly as the room moved. The door handle rattled again. She peered over the rim of the toilet bowl. There was still something there, some vestige. She flushed it, noticing that the chain seemed very far away. She shut her eyes as the roar of the cistern engulfed her.

The door handle rattled violently. She made to undo the bolt, then remembered the knitting needle was in the washbasin. Turning unsteadily, she snatched it up and put it in her pocket. With a supreme effort she undid the bolt and opened the door, just as her mother was about to hammer on it with her fist.

'Thank you!' Mrs Wickham barged in and slammed the door behind her.

Paula turned and faced the door of her room. The floor felt as if it was giving way. She put out her hand and grasped the banister, seeing her fingers take a grip but feeling nothing. The rail had no substance.

She tried to move forward and without wishing it to happen she was aware she was turning, seeing the stairs and the hall in front of her as she swayed. The knitting needle, only half-way in her pocket, fell out, bounced, then rolled into the gap between the carpet and the wall. She looked down, wondering where it had gone, knowing she should recover it. As she lowered her head she felt her body follow the direction of her gaze. She drifted forward in a long smooth sweep, seeing the hall come close as she fell forward.

12

It had started to rain. Richard hurried, running pigeon-toed to keep his boots from getting splashed. He was in uniform, with three stripes now and an aircrew flash. Before he reached the door Mrs Wickham opened it and put a finger to her lips, imploring silence.

He crept inside and she shut the door quietly behind him, leading him by the hand to the front room. The table was laid for tea. There were sandwiches, a special cake and jelly. Richard patted his hair and showed a proper facial concern as he asked Mrs Wickham, in a low voice, what exactly had happened.

'It was the cross woman has to bear,' she whispered, setting out plates and cups. 'I've laid ·mine down, thank God . . .'

Richard looked blank.

'That time of the month,' she said, and saw a glimmer of understanding. 'And she was having this *boiling* hot bath. It's not surprising she passed out.'

At the sound of a floorboard creaking she went to the door and slipped out into the hall. 'You look better,' she said brightly as Paula came down the stairs.

In the front room Richard was trying to control his

hair. He had a few strands at the crown that would never lie down for more than a few minutes at a time, no matter how much Brylcreem he slapped on. He stood in front of the mirror combing it flat as Paula and her mother talked out in the hall. When the hair was under control, for the time being, he flicked non-existent dandruff from his new stripes and flash.

'Surprise, surprise!' Mrs Wickham yelled, throwing open the front room door and startling him. He leapt away from the mirror and turned to greet Paula with a big smile. It died when he saw her pallor and the cold stare that conveyed nothing so much as disappointment. Suddenly he did not feel like much of a surprise. Paula made a thin sideways movement of her mouth and gripped the back of a chair. Mrs Wickham laughed heartily.

'Look at the birthday girl!' she cried. 'I'm sorry I couldn't wrap him up, but I didn't have a paper big enough!'

By a series of stiff, embarrassing stages they settled down to the birthday tea. Paula hardly communicated at all. She was near the window, and however much she moved her chair, she couldn't help seeing the shelter. That was where it had started. She tried not to see it. Her mother, anxious to keep the atmosphere light, behaved so artificially that she highlighted the tension in the room. Richard was bewildered.

When they had been seated for ten minutes and had eaten several of the sandwiches, Richard cleared his throat and said, 'Have you noticed anything?'

As he reached for a sandwich Mrs Wickham made a

dumb show for Paula, jabbing a finger at her sleeve. Paula stared at her, then leaned over and pulled the curtain across, shutting out the shelter. Richard and her mother stared at her.

'Sun's too bright,' she said.

Mrs Wickham looked at Richard, then back at Paula. 'It's raining,' she said.

Paula shrugged. 'Rain's too bright, then. Does it matter?'

She dropped her gaze to her plate. Mrs Wickham pulled Richard up in his chair, drawing his sleeve across in front of Paula. Paula stared at it.

'Good God,' she said. 'Sergeant Austen. I never thought of you as a Sergeant.'

'Neither did I,' he said, still bent awkwardly in front of her. He tapped the aircrew flash. 'Look.'

'He's the boy in blue you always wanted,' said Mrs Wickham, with a catch in her voice.

'Oh, for God's sake, Mother!'

'Oh, for God's sake,' Mrs Wickham echoed indulgently.

'You can't fly,' Paula told Richard as he sat down again. 'Your eyes are too weak.'

'My ears are all right.'

'You don't fly with your ears.'

'Radio,' he said. 'I'm a radio op.' He fumbled in his pocket, clearing his throat. 'I thought, I wondered . . .'

Mrs Wickham got up hurriedly and grabbed the teapot. 'I'll just freshen this tea,' she said, and hurried out of the room.

'As I'm going up, so is my pay,' Richard said as the

door closed. 'I wondered if we might –' He took a small square box from his pocket and put it on the table in front of Paula. 'Open it.'

She frowned at the box, taking off the lid. It was a wedding ring. It was the very last thing she expected. This was awful. Terrible. She was crying. 'Oh, Richard,' she managed. 'You are a wonderful person . . .'

'I wondered . . .' Richard's eyes shone, 'if we might get married now.' He smoothed his crown furiously as Paula picked up the ring and looked at it, turning it slowly.

'It's lovely,' she said. As Richard bent towards her she jerked vehemently away from him. 'But I can't. I'm sorry. I can't marry you. I can't marry anyone. I'm sorry.'

The ring fell on the table. She pushed back her chair and hurried out of the room, colliding with her mother, who had been listening at the door.

A month had gone past since the fighting with the Germans at the farm, and by now that incident had lost any special prominence as a memory. Time, plus the grind and forward surge of circumstances, flattened every event to insignificance. It did much the same to people, in Bob's view. In a way that he could not articulate, he felt there were times when B Company was like one creature, each man a component with no individual significance.

This was one such time. The company was huddled in pouring rain at the side of a French country road, identical to thousands of other French roads. They had fallen out for a smoke and were bunched around a lorry for shelter. They were oblivious to the distant gunfire, to the rain and even to their own discomfort. They concentrated on the only certainty, their next cigarette, lit by a match held out by another soldier, identically dirty, one fraction of the homogeneous huddle.

Leaning close to the side of the lorry, Second Lieutenant Gray took something from his pocket. Bob, standing near by, watched apprehensively. Captain Warburton came past at that moment, with Sergeant McCulloch squelching at his side.

'Must be in the blood of our ancestors,' Warburton said to Gray. 'French mud at this time of year. I think Monty's taking the scenic route.'

McCulloch turned and addressed the men in his usual bark, pointing off to the right. 'Dig in on the brow over there!'

Gray sidled over to Bob. 'Before you pick up your spade,' he said, handing Bob some lined sheets of notepaper with round, laborious handwriting on them, '"what" has an "h" in it.'

Bob considered that. 'Why, sir?'

'No reason. Like King's Regs.'

Bob looked at the pages, sliding them one over the other, keeping them out of the rain.

'Less corrections than last,' he finally said. 'Only about fifty. Wu-hot do you think, sir?'

'Not bad,' Gray said. 'Stick at it.'

'Oh I will, sir. I can do anything I put my mind to. I know that.'

Gray smiled with open warmth. 'There's certainly one thing you don't lack, Longman, and that's confidence. Have you heard from her yet?'

'No. But I'm determined to have my own letter ready when I do. I never showed you her picture, did I?'

Bob dug in through his cape, unbuttoning his battledress blouse and poking in his shirt pocket. He brought out the tattered clipping from the *Seaforth Gazette*, folded at Paula's picture. Even on the low quality newsprint, faded and dirty, her features stood out clearly. Gray stared at the picture for a moment. He smiled.

'So that's the girl I wrote to.'

'She's a bit of all right, sir, isn't she?'

Variations in the pattern of daily life would be hard to conceal in a household of only two women. The letter lying on Mrs Wickham's mat was a distinct change: the envelope, the handwriting, the frank mark. Nothing of that shape or description had landed on that mat before. Mrs Wickham picked it up, studied the flowing handwriting, held it up to the light. It was abruptly snatched away from her. Paula took it straight upstairs.

'Who's that from?' Mrs Wickham demanded. 'Whoever it is has got beautiful handwriting.'

The bathroom door slammed shut, shaking the whole house. Mrs Wickham moved quickly to stop one of her china ornaments slipping from the shelf. The bolt went on the bathroom door. There was an almost simultaneous thump on the front door, threatening to dislodge another ornament.

'Coal!' a voice shouted.

In the bathroom Paula sat on the lavatory seat and opened the letter. Reading it, she heard Bob's voice, exactly as it had been that last night they were together in the Blue.

'I love you Paula, I didn't know what the word meant till I met you. It was stupid and wrong of me to leave you like that. Please forgive me. The thought of you and the baby – my baby – keeps me alive. I am sending you as much of my pay as I can. Write to me soon. Your ever loving Bob.'

Outside, the coalman lumbered past the side of the house, whistling, bent low with a bag of coal on his shoulder. Mrs Wickham stood behind the curtain in the side passage, watching him. He stopped and expertly jerked the bag off his shoulder, then tipped the contents into the coal-hole.

'One,' Mrs Wickham murmured, not blinking.

She jumped at a commotion upstairs. Paula was shouting. Mrs Wickham ran out into the hall. It was as if the girl was up there with someone, shouting at someone. What was she saying? It's dead?

Mrs Wickham shouted: 'Paula? What is it?'

'It's too late!'

'You what?' Mrs Wickham ran upstairs and banged on the door. She tried the knob, but it was still locked. 'Paula? Paula?'

Beyond the door Paula moaned again. 'Why?' she cried. 'Why?'

Mrs Wickham turned, hearing the cheerful whistle of the coalman going along the side of the house again. She charged down the stairs and along the side passage, pressing her face to the window just as he jerked another bag from his shoulder and tipped it into the coal-hole.

'Two,' she panted. You had to watch them. You could trust nobody these days, nobody.

In the bathroom Paula was holding the letter between her hands as if it were a living presence, as though it was Bob himself.

'This is a joke, isn't it?' she said. 'One of your stories, isn't it? Another lie.'

There was the sound of Mrs Wickham coming up the stairs again. What was the girl saying, for God's sake? She heard her distinctly: 'You've been having a bloody good laugh together. I can hear you!'

Through the door Mrs Wickham demanded to know what was going on, and who Paula was talking to. This time when the coalman went whistling to the coal-hole she stayed where she was, rattling the handle of the bathroom door, shouting to Paula.

Inside Paula was gripped in a frenzy. Her fingers dug into the letter as she bumped around in the confined space, hitting the walls, knocking over the toilet brush, throwing the bath rack, the washing powder, the soap.

'She got rid of hers and she still went with you!' she shouted. 'Is that what you expect me to do? Well . . . Well . . .' She ripped up the letter and stuffed it into the lavatory. 'Love? I hate you! I hate you!'

She yanked the chain and when the lavatory didn't flush she jerked so hard the chain came off. She stared at it dangling from her hand. Half laughing, half sobbing, she clambered on to the lavatory seat and yanked the cistern lever. She slipped off the seat, stumbling and sliding down to the floor, her back pressed against the wall. The lavatory flushed. She saw the pieces of paper bobbing in the torrent. The expression on her face was one of sheerest pain, as if she had stuck a knife in herself.

Mrs Wickham stood back from the bathroom door, letting go the handle. She stared at the blank panels, hearing the dying flush.

The letter flap was rattling. Mrs Wickham shook herself and went down, holding on to the banister. She opened the door to the coalman, who was covered with coal-dust from his cap to his boots.

'Four bags, love.'

Mrs Wickham frowned at him. 'I counted three.'

'Four bags, love,' the coalman's eyes gleamed brightly in his black face.

She turned abruptly as the bathroom door was unbolted. She stared as Paula came down the stairs. The girl looked calm now, though in a way that was not normal. Her face was unnervingly, frighteningly calm.

At the foot of the stairs Paula stopped, her hands clasped placidly in front of her. 'I'm going to get married, Mother.'

For the moment Mrs Wickham was too distracted to keep her attention on the coalman. 'Who to?' she asked.

'Richard. Who do you think?'

'Congratulations,' the coalman said, the wrinkles of his grinning face etched with tiny seams of coal. 'Can I kiss the bride?'

Mrs Wickham turned and glared at him.

'Four bags, love,' he said.

She had the money ready. She stuffed it quickly into his grubby hand and closed the door. She turned slowly and faced Paula with her hand clutched to her heart.

'I counted three and I've paid him for four,' she said. 'I've never done anything like that in my life before. What on earth is going on?'

Paula still looked very calm and distant. 'On Saturday,' she said.

'What?'

'We're getting married on Saturday. On his next leave.'

13

Mrs Wickham was at the front gate, watching as an Austin Ten with ribbons attached drove up, its horn pipping. She waved furiously and ran back to the front door, pushed it open and called inside.

'Your Uncle Jack! Paula!'

Jack, a dedicatedly sunny man in his mid-fifties, got out of the car and stood grinning. He had a weary look beneath the shine, which was not helped by the stodgy effect of his brown hat perched squarely on his head. His wife, Enid, got out the other side, clutching a bunch of artificial flowers. They watched as Paula came along the path to greet them. She wore a dark green suit with a brown hat.

'Oh, yes,' Enid murmured, her lips as motionless as a ventriloquist's and slightly parted, to accommodate her prominent teeth. 'I see what all the hurry's about. There's a bun in that oven, all right.'

When Jack asked her how she could tell, she gave him a pitying look and went forward to embrace Mrs Wickham.

'Sarah, love, this is a happy day,' she beamed, her eyes cold above a pained smile. 'What are you crying for?'

Mrs Wickham wiped her eyes. 'I always saw her in white,' she said.

'Oh, Mother, for God's sake!' Paula snapped. She stared as Enid handed her the bunch of flowers. 'What are these?'

'They look like flowers to me,' her mother said.

'I made them myself,' Enid said. 'You can't be a bride without flowers. Keep them out of the wind.'

Jack came through the gate, still grinning. 'Pity you're in such a hurry,' he said to Paula, making his wife scowl. 'Never mind about wearing white. I could have got some petrol for the car as well.' He let out a shattering laugh at the women's expressions.

Twenty minutes later, outside the register office in Queen's Square, Richard watched a wedding party leave, six of them crammed into one car. He looked anxiously at his watch and patted the crown of his shiny hair, conscious of how exposed and awkward he must look standing there, open to the scrutiny of the queue forming at the fish stall. He looked up the steps to the door of the register office and saw the Registrar, a dour, lantern-jawed man in a grey suit. He was staring at Richard.

'You my eleven o'clock?' he called.

Richard nodded vigorously. 'Yes, sir.'

'Make sure she's not late.' The Registrar pointed to the stall. 'I shut at quarter-past to queue for my fish.'

A mile away, Uncle Jack pulled on the handbrake and shrugged at the women as the car rolled to a sharp halt. They were out of petrol.

'I thought you were joking,' Enid said.

'I was and I wasn't. I had no coupons. If she hadn't been in such a hurry . . .'

Enid elbowed him so hard he gasped. Mrs Wickham sighed and stared out of the window, her fingers drumming on her handbag. Only Paula, clutching her gaudy flowers, appeared to be calm. The calmness had never left her from the moment she had announced the wedding to her mother. Now, just as calmly, she said: 'I'm not pregnant.'

Her mother put on an affronted face. 'What a thing to say! Who's saying you are?'

'They are,' Paula said, nodding at her uncle and aunt. 'All but.'

Jack and Enid stared at each other, all shock and indignation. Paula looked as if she might laugh. Instead, she suggested they get out and push, if they wanted to get to the register office anywhere near the appointed time.

It took ten minutes to get the car to the top of the rise that swept clear downhill to Queen's Square. As the three women laboured the last few feet on to the level stretch at the top, Paula began to laugh. The other two, breathless, could see no cause for it.

'If I – if I were pregnant,' she gasped, 'this would do for it!'

Mrs Wickham was gathering breath to comment on the bad taste of the remark, when Jack stuck his head through the window and yelled 'All aboard . . . quick!'

The car was beginning to roll gently downhill. Mrs Wickham and Enid scrambled forward and jumped in. Paula remained where she was, her eyes momentarily distant. Jack roared with laughter as the two women threw themselves gasping on to the back seat.

'I don't know about the wedding,' Mrs Wickham said, 'this is more likely to get me to my funeral.'

'For God's sake!' Jack braked suddenly. 'Where's the bride?'

They looked through the back window. Paula was still at the top of the rise, standing in the middle of the road. From there she could see the ruined wing of Bank Top, where the bomb had dropped. Her calm began to go.

Meanwhile, in Queen's Square, the Registrar had appeared again at the door of the register office. He looked at the growing fish queue, and at the sizes of the slabs of fish being unloaded from the van from Grimsby. Then he looked at his watch.

'Three minutes,' he told Richard.

On the hill they were shouting at Paula to get into the car. Running to it, she lost a shoe and hopped back to get it. The car started moving again. Paula's hat fell off. She caught it, then jerked open the door and jumped in.

'You'll kill us all!' her mother wailed. 'Oh, my heart. Do you want to get married or not?'

Paula said nothing. Nothing at all. She sat back, fixing her hat, staring straight ahead as the car accelerated downhill, passing Bank Top, towards Queen's Square.

Outside the register office the Registrar was now staring at Richard. 'She's changed her mind,' he said flatly, and turned to lock the door.

Richard clapped his hair despairingly, watching the old man fumble with his keys. In desperation he fiddled with the winder of his wristwatch.

'You said quarter past,' he called to the Registrar.

'Takes ten minutes,' the man said, 'even if I crack whip a bit.'

'You're fast,' Richard said. 'I only make it eleven.'

The Registrar turned slowly and stared, peering at the wristwatch Richard was holding up for him to see. His brow furrowed. With stately indignation the man began to unshackle the ancient repeater from his waistcoat pocket. The process of checking was lengthy, involving the opening of the case once the watch had been released. That way precious seconds were gained. Richard glanced aside and saw Jack's Austin Ten roll to a stop by the fish stall.

One of the spectators in the queue was Bri, with Tiger at his side, keeping Vera's place while she went to get the bread. Just as Paula ran across to the register office, Bri looked along the road to the bread stall to see how close Vera was to getting served. When he turned round again, all he saw were the backs of the three women and the man hurrying over the pavement to the register office.

The Registrar was opening his watch when Paula turned up. He was about to take them into the register office when Paula took Richard aside.

'I want to talk to you,' she said.

The Registrar gaped at her. Mrs Wickham was too short of breath to say a word, but her expression was eloquent. She remonstrated, using her head and her arms.

'I haven't had the chance to talk to him,' Paula said, agitated, twisting her fingers together.

'You've only known him twenty years,' Mrs Wickham panted.

'You've got the rest of your life to talk to him, love,' Enid put in.

Grimly the Registrar opened the front of his gold repeater. Richard watched him, desperately flattening the hair at his crown. The moment of emergency produced sudden inspiration. Richard turned and spoke with an assertiveness he hadn't known he possessed.

'Will someone queue for his fish?'

Young Bri was idly watching the group by the register office, seeing one of them, Enid, come across and join the queue. His attention sharpened abruptly as he saw the face of the young woman standing by the man in the RAF uniform. He couldn't be sure at that distance, but . . .

He wandered out of the queue, getting closer to the wedding group. Tiger came after him. Bri turned and sternly pointed at the gap in the queue. 'Sit! Stay there, or I'll flatten you!' The dog went back to the queue and sat down.

By the register office steps Richard waited for Paula to say something. The delay had drawn a number of onlookers. But Paula didn't seem able to find words. When eventually she did speak it was in such a low voice Richard could scarcely hear her.

'I've been with someone,' she said.

Richard looked at her uncertainly, touching his hair.

'I'm not a virgin,' Paula explained.

Richard raised his hand to his hair again, but the

irritation on her face stopped him. His hand twitched instead.

'You'll be able to teach me, then,' he said, 'won't you?'

Paula blinked. 'You mean . . . you still want me?'

'I always have and I always will,' he said. 'I can't imagine marrying anyone else but you.'

The plain certainty in his voice brought on a rush of feeling in Paula. Whatever the cause was, friendship, affection, did it matter? She drew Richard towards her and kissed him passionately on the mouth.

'Middle of the square!' gasped Mrs Wickham, scandalized. 'You're supposed to leave that till afterwards!'

The Registrar, now that he was sure of getting his fish, became benign and expansive. 'Nay,' he said, waving an arm towards the register office. 'I don't think what happens in there really matters. Not these days.'

The children and other spectators delivered a spirited round of applause. Paula pulled away from Richard and looked down, startled to see Bri, who seemed dumbfounded.

'Hey!' he shouted. 'You're our Bob's girl!'

Paula glared at him. 'I am nobody's girl!' She linked arms with Richard. 'I'm his wife. Shall be.'

Paula and Richard turned and ran towards the register office. As Bri watched them go a stinging slap landed on his ear. Half stunned, he edged away, warding off another blow. It was Vera.

'I told you to stay in the queue!'

'I left the dog there!'

'You left the dog there!' Vera said, with withering scorn. She slapped him again and grabbed him by the jersey, pointing to where the dog cowered a couple of feet away. Then she moved her quivering finger to the fish stall, which was now nearly bare. 'You've lost our fish!'

Bri was struggling to get away from her. 'Our Bob's lost his girl!' he shouted. 'Stop them!'

'What are you on about?'

Bri pointed at the couple standing at the top of the register office steps. 'That's his girl!'

'Her and a hundred others,' Vera said.

Bri went on struggling and he began to cry, partly from the pain of the blows, partly from something he could not understand but could only feel as pure, aching grief.

'No,' he moaned, 'she's the one, he told me, he were mad about her – do something, stop them . . .'

'I will do something,' Vera said, dragging him away to the fish stall. 'I'll knock your block off.'

'I'll tell our Bob –'

'Our Bob! That useless lump.'

'He's not!' Bri started to cry even harder. 'He's not! He told me he were going to buy a car and be rich. What am I going to tell him about her?'

'Stop bawling, will you? We might just get a couple of scraps of coley.'

The dog nuzzled at Bri's legs. At the first contact of the wet nose Bri rounded on him. 'I told you to stay in that bloody queue!'

As they rejoined the queue Enid moved off, carrying a parcel of fish. She took it into the register office. At the door Mrs Wickham was straightening Paula's hat and fussing with her hair. Bri stopped crying as he watched them, a look of awe on his face.

'Are you going to get married?' he asked Vera.

'What? And have kids like you? Not bloody likely.' She fished out her handkerchief and shoved it at him. 'Here. Wipe the snot off your nose.'

The dog sidled in again behind Bri. The queue moved up. Vera sighed. They would get a few scraps, but it was all they could afford anyway.

Bob was sitting on the ground, reading to Arthur from the Army Bureau of Current Affairs pamphlet on the Beveridge Report.

'There are five giants that Beveridge says we must slay. The Giant of Want, the Giant of . . .'

'Ignorance,' Arthur prompted.

'That's me all right,' Bob said, frowning at the page.

McCulloch came up the road carrying a bulging potato sack. He put it on the ground and took out a handful of letters. Soldiers began moving towards him. Bob's attention strayed to the sack.

'The Giant of Sss . . . Sss . . . Oh bugger it!'

He hurled the pamphlet angrily away from him. Arthur retrieved it. 'Come on,' he coaxed, 'finish off the giants.'

Bob was watching McCulloch, who was besieged by soldiers now as he pulled mail out of the sack. Arthur pushed the pamphlet into Bob's hand. Bob set his teeth and glared at it.

'Sss . . .' He closed his eyes a moment, then looked at the page again. He shook his head.

'Squalor,' Arthur said.

'Squalor. I know that one, too.'

McCulloch was calling names and handing out mail, making crass jokes and deadly puns: 'Bollock! Sorry lad, I keep forgetting it's Pollock. Anderson, J. ... Holmes! I don't know what she's squirted in there – smells like a Hindu's jockstrap . . .'

Arthur looked towards McCulloch, then at Bob, indicating they go across. Bob shook his head; he wanted to finish the giants. As Arthur got up and moved off, Bob shifted his grip on the pamphlet, concentrating furiously.

'I . . . Ide . . .' His face cleared and he smiled. He had suddenly decoded the symbols for a sound that he had known most of his life. *He could see the word.* 'Idleness! Giant Idleness! Aye, I know you too, you bugger.' He pressed his finger to the page. 'D . . . Dis . . .'

Then he looked up, hearing his name. He stared at McCulloch.

'Longman,' he said pointedly, holding up a letter. 'Do you expect me to throw it?'

Bob got up, staring at the envelope. His heart began to pound.

14

The war ended. People celebrated briefly, then tried to regain the world they had lived in before. In small things the reversals seemed most pleasant: the disappearance of blackout curtains, for one. Their removal from Paula's room made it infinitely brighter, particularly in the mornings. The presence of a double bed, however, made the room much smaller than before.

Another blight which people were at pains to eliminate was the air raid shelter. On the morning that Uncle Jack was due to come round and dismantle Mrs Wickham's shelter, Richard stood by the bedroom window longer than he should, enjoying the sight of sunlight on the garden while he finished brushing his hair.

Paula was still asleep. As he put on his uniform jacket he listened to her soft breathing. She looked completely serene, far too comfortable to disturb. He picked up his bag, leaned across the bed and gently kissed her.

In the doorway he paused, looked at her again, then left, closing the door quietly. Paula had been awakened by the kiss, but she lay still with her eyes closed, taking in the first sounds. She could hear Richard close the front door, then his voice, dishearteningly cheerful as he always was in the mornings.

'Looks like you mean business, Jack.'

'What goes up must come down,' Uncle Jack called, and walked along the side of the house, whistling. Paula heard something heavy being dropped in the back garden. She stretched, taking her time over it, then threw back the covers and swung her feet out on to the floor. She rose slowly, her pregnancy looking huge in the nightdress.

At the window she watched Jack put down a crowbar beside a sledgehammer and other tools. Mrs Wickham appeared beside him. After a moment's preamble, muttering and pointing at the shelter, they both took hold of spades and began digging away the earth at one side of the shelter.

Paula put her feet into her slippers, snatched up her dressing-gown and went to the door. She moved quickly, too quickly for the time of morning. She hurried downstairs, doing up the dressing-gown. By the time she got to the back garden Uncle Jack was prising apart the corrugated side panels of the shelter.

'What are you doing?' Paula demanded.

'Planting potatoes,' Jack said. 'When we've got this down.'

'Get back inside,' Mrs Wickham said. 'It's freezing.'

Paula watched Jack push the crowbar between two more sheets of the shelter's wall. 'You can't do that!' she cried.

Her mother glared at her. 'What are you on about?'

'We might need it!'

'Need it?'

'The war's over, Paula,' Jack said. 'Good riddance to it, I say.'

He lunged at the front with his crowbar and the door sprang away, exposing the damp interior. Paula rushed forward and jumped inside. Her mother and uncle stared as she scrambled over the mattress on her knees. At the back of the bed, on a shelf made from bricks, were a Thermos flask and several books. She started pulling out some of the bricks.

'That baby's not going to stay inside the way you treat it,' Mrs Wickham said. 'Mark my words. What *is* she doing?'

'All clear, Paula!' Jack impersonated a siren. 'They've gone, love. You can come out now.'

Paula took out a bundle of letters from behind the bricks. She held them close to herself, snatched up a book and pushed the letters between the pages. She eased herself backwards out of the shelter, clutching the book.

Mrs Wickham stood shaking her head. 'I were funny when I had you –'

Jack nodded. 'You couldn't stop supping gravy.'

'– but you're downright peculiar.'

Jack peered. 'What have you got there?'

He was staring at the torn edges of the envelopes sticking out of the book. So was Mrs Wickham. As they watched Paula straightened, doing it too fast so the weight of the baby made her stumble. The book slipped and the letters fell out. Paula made a dive for them at the same time as her mother, who was doing nothing to hide her curiosity. She picked one up and stared for a full second at Bob's round childish handwriting.

'You shouldn't bend like that,' she chided, turning the envelope over.

'Give me that!' Paula screamed, snatching the letter away from her mother, cramming it with the others back into the book.

Jack smiled reassuringly at Paula. 'Your den, were it?' he said. 'I remember when you were little –'

Paula turned away and strode back into the house, clutching the book. Jack looked at Mrs Wickham.

'What were they?' he said.

'Nay,' she sighed, 'don't ask me. I'm only her mother. She's been getting one every month.'

Paula went upstairs and shut herself in the bathroom. By the lavatory bowl she shredded one of the envelopes and dropped it into the water. She moved to tear the letter it had contained, but she could not do that. She unfolded the pages, letting her eye settle on a well-remembered passage:

I went very bad after hearing from Vera about your marriage, but nothing keeps me down very long because I thought the register office is not the church . . .

And another:

Then there is the baby . . . Even though you never write to me I shall go on sending the money because I think every day . . .

She folded the letter again, flushed the lavatory and went to her room. Taking the key from its hiding place, she stuffed the book and the letters into the dressing-table drawer and locked it.

Later that morning, as Jack took a tea break before attacking the final stage of the demolition, and while Paula had her mid-morning nap in the front room, Mrs Wickham went upstairs to find out what was so precious about those letters.

They were most likely to be in the dressing-table drawer, which was locked, as she had expected, and Paula had found a new hiding place for the key. That scarcely mattered, though. Mrs Wickham knew every hiding place in that house, every last nook and cranny. She went to the door and began to work from the left, prepared to search every crack and crevice on the way back to where she started. She would find that key. It wouldn't be on top of the curtain rail, or under the bed, she'd used those before. Behind the dressing-table, the wood was loose . . . yes . . . there was something!

Paula slept uneasily. The awkwardness of her bulk had made her angle her spine too obliquely in the armchair. To counter that she had pressed down with both hands at the chair arms, dreaming she was climbing as she pushed down to shift the slant of her abdomen. One hand had slipped right down the side of the chair and was now trapped, adding a bizarre new twist to her dream. The heat of the coal fire on her feet had translated itself, in her subconscious, to warm water, which she had to tread across before she started climbing again – except that now she couldn't get across the water, because her hand was caught in a cleft in the rocks.

The ground seemed to give way and she had a sudden sensation of falling. She woke with a start, blinking, rescuing her hand and rubbing her numb fingers. For a moment she simply lay there, slumped in the chair, letting her senses return before she undertook the struggle to rearrange her body.

She listened to the clicking of the coals, the steady beat of the mantel clock, the distant sound of Uncle Jack hammering. There was another sound, above her. She pushed herself up in the chair, grunting with the effort, and tilted her head to listen. The sound was in her room.

As she went up the stairs she saw the bedroom door was open. She could see the wedding picture of herself and Richard, then the dressing-table, and then she saw her mother, sitting on the bed turning the pages of one of Bob's letters. The others lay around her on the bedspread. Mrs Wickham looked up, making no move to conceal what she was doing. Paula could not meet her eyes. She gripped the banister, hurried up the remaining stairs and strode into the bedroom.

'You've no right –'

'I've every right!'

'Give me those!'

'I'll give you those!' Mrs Wickham swept a bunch of pages on to the floor, then more, her face twisted with revulsion. 'I'll give you those!'

She got up off the bed, wiping her hands on her apron as if they were dirty. She stared through the window where Jack was working and whistling, dust rising from his efforts.

'It was in there, was it, that that thing was conceived?' She turned and glared at Paula. 'I wonder you can wake up in the morning and bear to look at it!'

Paula ignored her, crawling on the floor, gathering

up the scattered sheets of paper. Some had gone under the bed and she had to stretch to reach them. Her mother kicked one towards her.

'As if the shelter was a . . . I don't know what,' Mrs Wickham spluttered. 'What were you trying to do – have it as some kind of a monument to that thing?'

Paula struggled to her feet, clutching the papers in her clenched fists. 'Don't keep calling it that!'

'What shall I call it then – a bastard?'

Mrs Wickham wiped spittle from her mouth as Paula held up the crushed letters.

'It's not his! It's Richard's!'

'What do you take me for?' Mrs Wickham's voice was harsher and more violent than Paula had ever heard it. 'An even bigger fool than I've been?'

'It's true!'

'You're a liar!' Mrs Wickham wrenched a wad of papers away from Paula, one of them a money order, and tore them. 'Why should he give you money? Men like him don't give money for their own children, let alone anyone else's!'

'It's Richard's!'

'You can't stop lying, can you?' Mrs Wickham took on a bewildered look. 'I've brought you up right, I don't know what more –'

'Right, right, right!' Paula yelled. 'I *have* done the right thing! That's the trouble! I've always done what other people expected me to do! Always always always! I wish to God I hadn't!'

'Shut up!' Mrs Wickham snapped. She glanced through the window and saw Jack with his hammer poised, looking up at the window. 'Do you want the whole street to know what you are?'

The outburst had exhausted Paula. She sat on the bed, wincing at a jab of pain across her abdomen.

'Aye,' her mother nodded, unmoved, 'you're good at that, aren't you?'

Paula flew at her mother with such violence that she ran backwards, banging into the dressing-table, then the wall. She put up her arms to protect herself, but Paula turned away. She gathered the papers and put them in her bag.

'I wish it was his,' she muttered.

Mrs Wickham, misunderstanding, picked up the fallen wedding picture and set it back on the dressing-table. 'That's something you'll be wishing for the rest of your life.'

Paula looked at her as if she had never seen her before. 'You don't understand. You never will.'

'Oh, I do . . .' Mrs Wickham, for her part, was also seeing Paula as a stranger. 'You tried to tell me, didn't you? You pretended it was someone else and I was stupid enough to believe you.'

'You said you'd throw me out on the streets –'

'That's where you belong!'

They stared at each other. Something had shifted and snapped, some long-standing, all-forgiving link between them. Paula put her bag up on the bed and opened it. Her mother went downstairs.

Half an hour later Paula stood in the hall, buttoning her coat with trembling fingers, the jarring of anger and determination and fear making her feel sick.

She stopped, realizing she had put a button in the wrong hole. She undid the coat and started over. Her mother stood half-way down the stairs, watching. Jack watched, too, from the cover of the kitchen. When the coat was buttoned Paula stood still for a moment, looking at nothing.

'Well, go if you're going,' Mrs Wickham said.

Paula stooped and picked up her bag. As she straightened, a spasm of pain sliced across her belly. She gulped, glancing at her mother. Mrs Wickham stared back, her face stony with disbelief.

'Just started, has it?'

On a final surge of temper and hatred Paula jerked open the front door, went out and slammed it so hard several china ornaments fell off the shelf. One of them smashed. Jack came out to help pick up the pieces.

'Where's she gone?' he asked.

Mrs Wickham stood up, a hand on her back. 'Make me a cup of tea, Jack.'

He stared at her. 'In your kitchen? You've never asked me to do that before!'

He watched her turn slowly and shuffle into the kitchen, her customary bouncing vigour gone. For the first time, he could see signs of an old woman in her. She waited for him to come in and nodded at the tea caddy.

'Two spoons, level, and half for pot,' she said, as she dropped into a chair.

15

The Neufeld Detention Camp was part of a German military prison camp, used now by the British to house German prisoners of war. It was a bleak collection of huts connected by muddy paths and surrounded by a high wire fence, set in open countryside fifteen miles south-east of Regensburg and fifty miles north of Munich. The best that Bob and the others in B Company could say about the place was that it was a change from France. The duties, on the other hand, were much less hazardous, and could even be enjoyable.

In defiance of fortune and the wishes of certain senior soldiers, Bob was now a Corporal with minor administrative and clerical duties. The job was agreeable, Bob's chances of being killed were now hugely reduced, and the work gave him an opportunity to refine his talent for manipulating people.

On a damp Monday morning, anxious for a hot cup of tea in the administration hut before the day's grind, he pushed open the door and took a swift look before he went in. It was a simple precaution, one he exercised whenever he could; it meant he was less likely to walk into a surprise. This morning he saw the usual drab collection of tables, benches and chairs, the flaking paint on the walls, the rot along the window ledges. It was an admin hut like a million others. There was a sign of movement in Lieutenant Gray's office at the far end, and the new clerk, Eva, was at a table near the door, typing on an old Adler with her fingers poking out of threadbare mittens. She was an attractive young woman, her large brown eyes emphasized by the malnutrition that shaded the looks of most German civilians by that time. She had a fetching smile, and Bob had noted that she used it without a trace of guile.

As he stepped inside, Arthur Spence was moving a rickety kerosene heater closer to Eva's table. She smiled gratefully and Arthur smiled back before he quickly looked away.

'You're not supposed to smile at them, Spence,' Bob snapped.

Eva frowned while Arthur, flustered, knocked over one of the heater's cover panels. Bob moved towards Eva's table and stopped. His air of authority was reinforced by the sharp creases in his uniform and the glittering of his cap badge.

'Monty says nothing about winking, though,' he added.

He gave Eva an outrageous stage wink. She grinned and even laughed a little as Arthur fumbled at the heater.

'Come on, Arthur,' Bob coaxed, 'vink. She fancies you.'

Sergeant McCulloch came in, coldly eyeing the tableau before him, maintaining his customary disdain for Bob, which was much more pointed now that Bob had been promoted. He jerked his head at Eva.

'What's she doing here?'

'Someone's got to type those forms,' Bob said easily. 'She's been vetted.'

'Who by?' McCulloch asked snidely. 'You?'

A door at the opposite end of the hut opened and a batch of shabby prisoners were led in.

'Her husband was killed by the Nazis,' Bob said.

He moved away to where the new arrivals were huddling and looking lost. McCulloch gave Eva a cold, peremptory glare before he moved off.

Bob was responsible, among other things, for processing prisoners at the stage where Nazi allegiances were deduced from their answers to War Department questionnaires. With Sergeant McCulloch he set about getting the prisoners seated at desks and tables and handing out the questionnaires. One man, an officer, narrowed his eyes at Bob as he handed him his form.

'We have met before,' the man said.

Bob looked and nodded, acknowledging no more than the fact that the man had spoken. But he did remember him. He was Captain Karl von Berner, who had walked into the courtyard of the farm – it seemed an age ago – and asked for permission to recover his wounded men. As Bob made to move along, von Berner held up his questionnaire.

'This is a waste of time,' he said. 'I was never a Nazi.'

'Then you'll have no trouble filling in the form,' Bob said.

'I am afraid I will.'

Their eyes met, a tiny collision of wills, then von

Berner smiled faintly and held up his ink bottle. It was empty.

Later, as the prisoners were lined up on the open ground between huts and were fed soup and rye bread, Lieutenant Gray emerged from his office to stretch his legs. That first letter to Paula, and teaching Bob to write, had led to him feeling part of the whole affair. He knew that – according to Bob – the money orders were getting through. Wasn't the baby due now? Bob improvised smoothly and said that the baby was in fact a little late. He'd heard nothing, and was hazy about dates, but writing to her made it real, convinced him it was happening. During that part of their exchange Karl von Berner had been scrupulously mopping up the remains of his soup with a scrap of bread, his head at a tense listening angle.

'What are you going to call the baby?' Gray said, then looked round sharply, noticing how close von Berner was standing.

There was the slightest moment of tension, then von Berner made a curt nod of acknowledgement, one officer to another, and moved away. When Gray looked at Bob again he saw the bafflement on his face.

'Well, you must have thought about a name.'

'No, sir,' Bob said.

'Well, you better had. If it's on the way.'

That afternoon at five, Eva came and stood before Bob's tidy desk. She put her pass in front of him to be stamped, as it had to be, twice, every day. Bob looked up and smiled at her. Somewhere in her presence, in the combination of her clear skin and the precise depth of her eyes, he detected an echo of Paula. Or thought he did.

Breathing loudly on his rubber stamp, he banged it down on the pass, leaving a faint blue trace. He examined the imprint for a second, deliberately looking beyond it, taking in Eva's tattered coat and her cracked shoes. Before, it had never occurred to him that German civilians had been brought to a bare level of existence, or that they could look so precisely like the poor people in Seaforth.

He initialled the pass with a flourish and handed it back, noticing that Arthur, at his own desk, was raptly studying the elegant line of Eva's neck.

'Vell, give her a vink, Arthur!'

Arthur was immediately covered in embarrassed confusion. He blinked at Eva and blushed deep pink. At the door she laughed.

''Wiedersehen,' she said.

'Vinkersehen,' Bob retorted.

Eva's laughter left her when she saw McCulloch look up from a desk at the other end of the hut. He glared at her in the same imperious way he had done earlier, then said something to Lieutenant Gray, who was standing near by. Eva hurried out.

'You're in there, Arthur,' Bob said.

'Don't be stupid.' Arthur fussed with the paperwork piled in front of him. After a moment, not wishing to move off the topic of Eva, he said, 'She hates the Nazis. But she thinks we don't understand. Not every German was a Nazi, but −' He looked up and saw Bob was grinning at him.

'You're not doing that badly, are you?' Again Arthur looked uneasy. 'Trouble with you, Arthur, is you're not a closer. Look. Fair do's. You've helped me with the reading. I'll teach you the secret of the chat.' Bob winked. 'The way to a woman's – hey up . . .' He broke off as Karl von Berner entered. 'Yes, Captain?'

Von Berner handed him a requisition sheet. 'The cleaning party needs more materials.'

Bob studied the sheet. 'Do they eat soap?'

'Well . . .' Von Berner shrugged. 'It tastes almost as good as the bread.'

Bob pulled a stores requisition across the desk and picked up his pen. He still savoured writing, the physical feel of it, the nib going into the ink, got pleasure from the neat pattern forming on the page. He still felt a great sense of release that he no longer had to go through the endless subterfuges he had used when he couldn't read or write.

'Congratulations, Corporal,' von Berner said. 'I couldn't help hearing . . . Is it your first?'

'Yes,' Bob said curtly. 'Will be.'

'Children are the most important thing in life.'

Von Berner took a photograph from an inside pocket and offered it. Bob took it and held it to the light. It was a picture of three girls, the eldest about nine.

'Since a year,' von Berner said quietly, 'I have not seen Kristina and Ilse.'

Bob frowned a question at him as he handed back the picture. Von Berner turned his head aside as he put it away.

'Sophie, she was killed. In an air raid.'

Bob stamped the form and handed it across. 'I'm sorry,' he said.

Von Berner thanked him. As he went away Bob felt a twinge of pity. Then he forgot him as he felt the urge to write another letter to Paula. He felt, more strongly than he had ever felt anything in his life, that he *was* already a father, or about to become one.

A newspaper blew against Paula's legs as she came out of the telephone box. She kicked the paper away, changed her grip on the suitcase and walked along the road with her head bowed against the wind. She had no idea what she was doing, where she was going. On the telephone Julie's mother had been offhand, saying Julie, who had been on the same bench at Winter's, was on shift and wouldn't be back until much later. What would she have said to Julie, anyway? Calling her had been an impulse, an attempt to talk to someone.

The one thing she was certain about was she couldn't go back. Not to her. Not to that house, with the shelter a constant reminder and every time she went into the bathroom . . . Part of her was terrified, but wasn't part of her glad to be out of there? Already feeling – how on earth did I go on living there?

The wind buffeted her every time she turned a corner. The case banged at her legs. One of the catches was loose and snagged her stockings. Each spasm across her stomach was more painful than the one before; the last two had snatched the breath from her.

A weakening in her legs warned her another was coming. It flashed diagonally from somewhere under her ribs to her groin. She caught her breath and let the case slip from her fingers. Something in the pain, in its depth, reminded her of the time in the bathroom when she had used the knitting needle.

A wave of nausea washed over her. It left her cold and shivering. She picked up the case again. Ahead of her she saw another telephone box. She walked towards it, seeing a man come out as she approached. She pulled out her diary and the wind blew it from her fingers. The man sprinted past her and trapped it with his foot. He picked it up and brought it to her. She saw his little frown of concern.

'Are you all right?'

'Yes,' she said, dry-mouthed, hearing herself croak. 'Thank you.'

She got herself into the telephone box and put down the case. The wind had put tears in her eyes and she had to blink before she could read the numbers in her book. She dialled slowly and was surprised at how close the answering voice sounded.

'Hello?' She cleared her throat. 'Sergeant Austen, please.'

'Sorry,' the operator said, 'Flight Sergeant Austen is on operations. Who's that speaking?'

Paula identified herself, and added that she believed the baby might be starting. The operator chatted to her – how lovely, she would tell Sergeant Austen.

'I don't know,' Paula said quickly. 'It might be a false alarm. Tell him to call me. Not at home, I've left . . . Tell him he mustn't whatever he does call me at home.'

'Where are you, love?'

'Mafeking Park, Seaforth.'

'Which road?'

Which road? Paula stared wildly through the glass, first on one side, then the other. Vaguely she registered somebody waiting to use the phone, his coat flapping in the wind.

'Are you there? Mrs Austen?'

Paula jammed the receiver to her ear. 'There's a public house,' she said, 'in Mafeking Park. The Blue Anchor. I'll go there. If anything happens they can tell him . . .'

Towards tea time that evening, young Bri Longman decided to give Tiger a few overdue obedience lessons on the pavement outside Jacko's second-hand shop. The plan of procedure was for Bri to throw a stick, then yell at the dog to stay. Tiger did as he was told, but with terrible reluctance, gazing desperately at the stick where it lay, whining low in his throat. The training session had been going for five minutes when Dora, Bri's little sister, appeared at the end of Kitchener Street and shouted to him.

'She says if you don't come *now*, you'll get nowt!'

Bri was unmoved. 'Bread and scrape? You can have my share.' He flicked a half-crown in the air and caught it. At the same moment he noticed the dog was about to make a run for the stick. 'No!'

Tiger stopped in his tracks and whined. Dora appeared at Bri's side and stared accusingly at the coin he kept flipping. She asked him where he got it. Bri turned and nodded towards Jacko, who was removing unredeemed pledges from the window at the end of the day's trading.

'I've taken over our Bob's business,' Bri explained to his sister. He nodded towards Jacko again. 'He says

I'm smart enough to follow in his footsteps. Pity there's no more bombs.'

With the air of one dispensing largesse, he took a handful of cake crumbs from his pocket and offered them to Dora. As she was about to take them he drew his hand back, stuffed half the crumbs in his mouth and threw the rest to the dog.

'You mean bugger!' Dora yelled.

'Well, you always get everything.' Bri tossed the coin again. 'You're not going to get a chip, not a single scrap –'

Dora reached out and snatched the coin, then screamed as Bri cut off her escape.

'Get her, Tiger,' he snarled. 'Kill kill kill!'

Dora ran screeching with Bri and the dog after her. Then she looked up and stopped dead. Bri grabbed her, then followed her gaze. The dog stopped behind them, shifting from paw to paw, growling uncertainly.

'It's her,' Bri said.

At the end of the street was Paula, squatting over her suitcase, doubled over with pain.

'Telephone,' she gasped. 'Get a doctor. Ambulance . . .'

'Box on corner's broken,' Bri said.

He came near, his sister and the dog close behind him. A spasm of pain tore through Paula and she cried out.

'Get someone!'

Bri turned to Dora. 'Get Mum! Quick!' At the instant of issuing the order he remembered the half-crown. He grabbed Dora as she ran off and twisted her wrist to force her to release the coin. It dropped into his palm and he shoved her away.

'Go on!' he shouted at her. 'Quick!'

16

Kitchener Street, normally deserted at that hour, was buzzing with people as Paula was shown into number 18, faint and confused, hardly conscious of where she was. Bri and Dora came behind her, giggling with excitement, the dog running in and out at their feet. Men in braces, some with jam at the corners of their mouths, stood gaping, spectators at what was essentially women's business. Miss Thwaites's antennae had brought her swiftly to the scene. She stood next to Fred Spence, her face stiff with distaste, watching as Sal Longman helped her guest over the doorstep.

'I never thought I'd live to see this,' Miss Thwaites muttered. 'Brazen as they come!'

Sal was in her element. 'Come on, love,' she soothed, taking Paula by the elbow. 'Mind the step. Kettle, Dora. Get Mrs Thomas.'

The name of Mrs Thomas spread down the street like a grass fire. Her whereabouts became the topic of well-intentioned misinformation and urgent conjecture. She was a woman in regular demand in an area where conventional midwifery services cost more than people could afford, or at any rate more than they were willing to pay. Mrs Thomas had the God-given skills, it was widely believed, that only a few women were ever granted, innate skills which no doctor possessed.

In the bare, cold interior of number 18 Paula was put on a pull-down bed in the downstairs room, and screened by a trestle hung with washing. Her skirt and underclothes were removed with a minimum of ceremony and a blanket was thrown over her.

One neighbour, Joan, brought in a scuttle of coal, while another, Mary, made newspaper twists to build up the base of the spiritless fire flickering in the grate.

'It's Dr Hardy, Albany Road,' Paula said through gritted teeth.

'Nay, love,' Sal said, 'it's not worth spending money on a doctor when you can have Mrs Thomas – in't that right, Mary?'

'She's the best,' asserted Mary, a woman who could probably not imagine the best of anything.

'Provided you get her early enough in the day,' Joan added.

'What she loses is not worth keeping,' Sal said.

Paula sat up sharply. She looked terrified. 'I want Dr Hardy!'

The women gathered round her as she howled sharply with pain.

'She wants Dr Hardy,' Sal repeated.

The door opened abruptly and Mrs Thomas walked in, carrying a bulky carpet bag. She was about fifty, firmly built, with arms as thick as the average woman's legs. Her face was heavy-featured and built for frowning, and her expression as she crossed to the bed showed just what she thought of Dr Hardy. Sal moved back deferentially.

'You mean,' Mrs Thomas said, 'they dragged me

out of *Mrs Miniver* for nothing! I haven't had such a good cry for months.' She looked squarely at Paula. 'Dr Hardy would cost you twice as much, and I'm here and he's not.'

She took Paula's hand, and as she did Paula cried out again with pain.

'There, precious, there, let's have a look-see . . .' Mrs Thomas pushed aside the blanket and examined Paula's abdomen with cold, firm hands. Then she spread her legs as if she were opening curtains. 'Ah . . .' She peered, putting her face down close. 'You've got a good head there. This one's easy, precious . . . come out like a cork from a bottle . . .' – Mrs Thomas looked up and winked at Sal – '. . . to coin a phrase.' She winked again and returned her attention to Paula. 'Now breathe, breathe . . .'

Sal opened Paula's bag and rummaged inside. In a compartment at the back she found money. She took it and handed some to Bri, with a whispered instruction. He hurried away. As she closed the bag she caught sight of the sheaf of letters and money orders.

It was ten minutes to closing time and Dick Moxham was calling last orders when Bri ran into the Blue Anchor and put an empty bottle on the bar.

'Mrs Thomas's medicine, please.'

'What?' Dick stared down at Bri. 'Another lot? Isn't it out yet?'

Miss Thwaites, standing by the bar, watched Dick refill the bottle. She leaned across to Fred Spence and told him the young woman had identified herself as a Mrs Austen. Fred asked if there was a Mr Austen.

'What do you think?' Miss Thwaites said sourly. 'Bob Longman's like a dog that can't pass a lamp post. Even when he's not here he's leaving his mark.'

Beer sloshed from the pint Sue was pulling as she leaned across sharply to address Miss Thwaites and Fred.

'If it weren't for him,' she announced loudly, 'you lot would have nothing to talk about!'

The place went quiet. People stared. Dick made a show of laughing as he came back with Mrs Thomas's bottle.

'Nay,' he said to Sue, 'you wouldn't have wanted him, would you?'

Sue banged the pint down so hard that half of it slopped on to the bar. 'Yes!' she yelled. 'Yes, I would! He's worth all the lot of you put together! I wish –'

Tears filled her eyes suddenly and her voice caught. Cupping her hands to her face, she turned and ran to the back of the pub. Young Bri paid for the bottle and left, wondering again at the fluctuations and violent emotions of adult life. Once or twice he had wondered if he really wanted to grow up just to go through all that.

When he got back to number 18 Vera had just got home from the factory. She was standing by the bed in her outdoor coat and her turban, taking in the scene. Paula lay back on the bed panting, her legs awry. Her face was covered with sweat and she looked barely conscious. Sal and Mrs Thomas both looked exhausted. They also had the glaze of drink.

'It was doing fine,' Sal explained. 'Then the poor

pet stopped coming.' She gazed down between Paula's legs. 'It doesn't want to come into this wicked world, do you?'

'You can't blame it,' Mrs Thomas said, wearily shaking her head.

Vera turned away and took off her coat. As she did she caught two things in rapid sequence: she saw Sal frown at Bri to hide the bottle, and she saw the bottle. She hung up her coat, snatched the bottle off Bri and flung it into the fireplace. The sound of it smashing seemed to rally Paula. Her eyes fluttered and she began pushing again.

'What is it?' Vera demanded.

Mrs Thomas looked at her cautiously. 'I think . . .' The big woman motioned with her hands, which were trembling. 'I think it's the cord that's trapped. I just can't get at it.'

'Tell me what to do,' Vera snapped. 'I delivered Dora. Tell me what to do!'

Guided by Mrs Thomas and a good measure of her own instinct, Vera cupped a hand gently under the baby's slippery head. She probed with her other hand and felt the hard thickness of the cord across its shoulder. Extending her fingers with great gentleness, she found a couple of inches of slack in the cord and raised it, at the same time turning the child. It moved with a wet, sucking sound, making Paula's whole body shudder. Vera passed the loop over the little head, feeling the cord go slack at once.

'I think I got it!'

She slipped her curved hand across the baby's neck and shoulders to be sure.

'I got it free . . .' She looked up at Paula. 'Now push. Push. Harder. Go on, love.'

As Paula made her hardest effort yet to expel the child from her body, Richard Austen was standing at the bar of the Blue Anchor, talking to Dick Moxham. Sue was standing nearby, pale and tired-looking, putting on her coat.

'I'm looking for a Mrs Austen,' Richard said.

Dick looked baffled. 'Mrs Austen?'

'She's . . .' Richard swallowed nervously, glancing at the staring faces around the bar. He patted down his hair at the crown. 'She's having a baby.'

'Oh!' Dick's face cleared. 'You mean Bob's –'

Sue trod on Dick's foot so hard she almost broke a toe. He gulped, got the point, and leaned forward across the bar, setting his teeth a moment to cope with the pain. He smiled stiffly at Richard and told him he should go to number 18 Kitchener Street. Richard repeated the address, put on his hat and left.

He ran all the way down the dark street. He was unable to see the numbers – then he heard a sharp little howl that faltered, stopped, then broke into the full, unmistakable, complaining wail of a newly-born baby. Richard stopped by the door, trembling. He took off his hat and completely forgot to pat his hair. He knocked, waited a couple of seconds, then opened the door and walked in.

The baby had been washed and was being wrapped in a towel by Vera, helped by Joan. They paused and stared at Richard as he looked at the red, howling features of his child. A huge smile spread across his face. Vera had no need to ask who he was.

There was a sharp knock at the door. Bri opened it. Jacko, Dick Moxham and Fred Spence were there, carrying bottles.

'What is it?' Fred asked, coming half-way into the room.

'A girl,' Vera told him.

There was a suppressed commotion as the men came in and took turns to peer at the baby, which Vera held on to as if it were her own. Richard sat down by Paula, who was asleep. He took out his handkerchief and wiped her forehead gently. Bri and Dora put cups on the table as the bottles were opened. Sal, having been warned by Vera not to crowd the baby, shook her head with a heavy sigh.

'When you have a difficult passage,' she said, 'you have a difficult life.'

'Aye, that's true,' Mrs Thomas said.

'And by, she were difficult.'

'She were that,' chimed in Mrs Thomas.

Vera threw them a look of sheer scorn, but they were too busy rewriting history to notice.

'I'd hate to think what would have happened if I hadn't been here,' Mrs Thomas sighed.

Richard looked at Vera. 'I thought you were the midwife.'

Mrs Thomas gave Vera a bleary, patronizing smile. 'Vera here were very helpful,' she said.

The baby had drowsed for a couple of minutes, but now it cried out again, and Paula woke up. She looked about her, only her eyes moving as she took her bearings, scanning the dingy room for her baby. Her hair was matted and tangled with sweat and her skin was the colour of candle-wax, yet Richard thought she had never looked more beautiful. He watched in silence, enraptured.

At the window Sal had pulled back the curtain, letting a few people gathered outside look in and see the small bundle in Vera's arms. One of the people standing there was Sue. She craned her neck, smiled wanly for a moment, then walked off slowly down the street.

Vera brought the baby to the bed. Richard was suddenly overcome; he stood up and thanked everybody for their kindness towards his wife and his child. Fred Spence, having toasted the infant more times than he could now remember, asked what they were going to call her. Richard started to speak, then stopped. He sat down again and nodded to Paula.

'We're calling her Carol,' she said, her voice surprisingly strong. 'But I'd like – I'd like her middle name to be Vera.'

'Yes!' Richard said, grinning.

'Don't be daft,' Vera said, turning away sharply.

Fred raised his glass, preparing a revised toast. 'Carol Vera –' He stopped and frowned at Richard. 'What *is* thy name, lad?'

'Austen.'

The assembled company, roughly in unison, toasted the health and long life of Carol Vera Austen.

17

It was a frosty night and so still that the smallest sound could be heard distinctly. Bob walked along the outside of the perimeter wire, moving quickly to keep warm, his boots crunching on the grass and frozen earth. He checked one sentry, then walked off smartly to the next post. Half-way between the two he saw a movement near the wire on the inside of the camp. He stopped, drew his handgun and crept forward. There was another movement and Karl von Berner stepped into the perimeter light, his hands raised.

'Get inside!' Bob told him.

Von Berner lowered his hands. He took a step closer, almost touching the barbed wire. 'You stirred things in my head about the children,' he said, ignoring the order. 'They are in the east, in Magdeburg, in the Russian sector . . .'

He smiled bleakly and brought up his hand. It hovered in the air, then he closed it tightly round a spike on the wire. His smile faded, but he showed no sign of pain. He drew back his hand and looked at the blood welling from his palm. In the harsh artificial light it glistened dark purple.

'Is a cigarette possible?' he said.

Bob took out a packet with three in it. He passed one through the wire. Von Berner lit it.

'Put that light out!' the sentry yelled.

'All right, Midge!' Bob called back.

Von Berner thanked him for the cigarette. 'What did you do before the war got you, Corporal?'

Bob lit his own cigarette, took a deep drag and let the smoke out slowly. It felt a long time ago. He could dismiss what he used to be. He shrugged and said, 'I found things on bomb sites.'

Von Berner moved fractionally closer to the wire, his voice quieter than before. 'Germany is now the biggest bomb site in the world.'

There was something more than bitterness in his tone. Bob detected it and waited.

'Museums, art galleries, everything was bombed,' von Berner said. 'Banks . . . Currency moved.' He dragged on the cigarette. 'I know where there is a big fortune.'

Bob gazed for a moment at the smoke swirling around the light above their heads. 'Small fortune,' he said.

'Is that what you say? A small fortune.' Von Berner tilted his head, testing the sound of it. 'How British. It's not far from here. In the forest, near where I was caught.'

'Buried treasure,' Bob said, keeping his expression neutral, his voice flat.

'American dollars.' Von Berner smiled.

Bob returned the smile. 'Pull the other one.'

'The other one? Excuse me?' Von Berner frowned, searching Bob's face. 'You think it is a fairy story but I can prove –'

'Get inside!' Bob snapped. He stamped out his cigarette and put his hand on his gun. 'Go on! *Schnell! Schnell!*'

He smiled to himself, watching von Berner hurry back to the hut and go inside. As the door closed he went on staring at the hut for a moment, then stepped away from the wire, smiling again, and moved off to the next sentry post. In that other life he'd once led he could just have been stupid enough to fall for that.

At mid-morning Eva was typing steadily, the only person working in the admin hut, because the post had arrived. Lieutenant Gray was opening a parcel in his office, Sergeant McCulloch was poring over a letter at his desk, and Arthur Spence, for Bob's benefit, was reading aloud a letter from his father.

'"I have never known anything like it, son, even in Mafeking Park,"' he read. '"I could have dropped through the floor. I was almost calling her Carol Vera –"'

Bob snatched the letter and stared at it, amazed. '"Longman,"' he read, and looked at Arthur, his eyes wide. 'I'm a father.'

'But she's married,' Arthur said, 'To someone else. Look.' Arthur looked round, realizing he had practically shouted. Eva was staring. So was McCulloch. Lieutenant Gray, holding a cake he had just unpacked, was looking out from his office doorway. 'Bloke called Austen,' Arthur said, more quietly now. 'Look. She's Carol Vera Austen.'

In the silence Bob and Arthur realized that Lieutenant Gray had heard, and he had understood. He put down the cake and came out of his office. Bob swallowed hard, meeting his eyes.

'She, ah, didn't get your letter, sir. In time I mean. She were desperate. In the club. Grabbed hold of the first bloke. Wartime job. You know . . .' Bob glanced at the letter. 'In Kitchener Street. In our house. What does that tell you? It'll be sorted. It's a bit of a mess, but I'll sort it.'

Gray gazed thoughtfully at the rafters for a moment. 'I think "mess" is rather an understatement.' He looked at Bob. 'But I wouldn't be at all surprised if you did sort it.'

'Sort it?' McCulloch shook his head in disbelief. 'I thought you had your head screwed on, Longman. I'd let him have the bastard.'

Bob didn't think. He just said it. 'I love her,' he said. This ought to have produced jokes, ribald laughter, but there was such force, such a challenge in the words, it led to a silence. Then Lieutenant Gray clapped his hands three times. 'I think this deserves one of those miracles my mother does with dried egg,' he said.

There were cheers as he brought the cake from his office and sliced it with his pocket knife. Arthur gave a piece to Eva and the warmth of her smile smothered him in confusion. Bob, buoyant on the news from England, winked lavishly at both of them, making Eva laugh and almost choke on a bite of cake.

It was the first impromptu party at Neufeld Camp, and its effects stayed with Bob long after it had been abandoned and they all went back to work. In the afternoon, as he organized a working party with Arthur and a couple of other soldiers, he was still bubbling over with the effects of his new notion of himself.

'Vera's our family name,' he explained to Arthur, 'that's why she chose it, it were my grandmother's name, at least I think she were my grandmother – you never quite know where you are in Mafeking Park, do you?'

'You don't in your house,' Arthur said.

Karl von Berner, who was on the working party, picked up the mood and stood smiling.

'Good news?' he called.

'It's a girl,' Bob told him.

'Congratulations!'

There was real warmth in the German's smile. He wasn't a bad bloke, Bob thought – they were both fathers. In a little burst of exuberance he offered the German a cigarette, then gave him the whole packet.

On the map in Seaforth Town Hall – unchanged since 1938 – Mafeking Park is designated a slum clearance area. The only clearance ever carried out had been done by Hitler. Across the canal, and a little way from the factory belt, is an area marked, appropriately, grey. These houses were not on the right side of the park, but they were, at least, on the right side of the canal. They were skilled workers' houses, foremen's houses: through terrace, not back to back. The lavatories were outside, but each house had its own, with a scrap of yard at the back.

It was towards one of these houses, 15 Roberts Avenue, that Richard was walking on a bright day in 1946. He was so preoccupied he nearly bumped into a woman coming the other way. He swerved around her and muttered an apology.

'All right,' she said. Seeing his uniform and kitbag she added, 'Got long?'

'Forty-eight hours.'

He let himself into the narrow hallway and closed the door, hearing the echo. Practically the entire floor area was covered with linoleum, which seemed to bounce sounds right through the house.

'Paula? Carol?'

He stuck out his arms at the elbows and made a noise like an aeroplane, then stopped and listened. The place was quiet.

He went through to the sparsely furnished back room. A baby's rattle lay on the single square of rug. He picked it up and shook it gently, his face taut as he glanced through the back window. He put down the rattle with a trembling hand and moved to a small table that possessed, for Richard, the properties of a haven. On it lay a circuit board, a wiring diagram, coils of wire, a soldering iron, a number of valve bases and valves – diodes, pentodes, triodes. He pulled over a cardboard box with RAF DEFFORD marked on the side and from it he lifted out, with great care, a cathode ray tube.

The very act of handling the tube seemed to calm him. He sat down, holding it between his palms, glancing past it to the wiring diagram.

He was not sure how long he had worked on the circuit before Paula came home. It had certainly been an hour and was probably longer. The work always drew him in and absorbed him until he was practically a part of the process. At the sound of the front door he raised his head and listened as the pram was wheeled into the hallway. The door closed quietly, and a moment later Paula tiptoed into the back room.

'Oh!' She clapped a hand to her mouth. 'You're here!'

'Of course I'm here,' he said, getting up. His voice was sharper than he meant it to be.

'Ssh!' She kissed him but he pulled away. Paula stared at him.

'I've been here an hour,' he said. 'More. Where've you been?'

'Getting Carol to sleep,' Paula said, noticing how he was trembling.

'Where?'

'Mafeking Park. You know how dotty Vera is about her.'

Richard took a deep shaking breath. 'Why?'

'Why?' Paula frowned. 'You know why.'

Richard strode out to the hall and drew the blanket away from the sleeping baby. Paula watched him, told him not to wake her. He rounded on her.

'You're all dolled up,' he said.

'Of course I am.'

'Have you been to see him?'

Paula stared. 'He's overseas.'

Richard swallowed. 'You know who I mean, then?'

'What is this? What are you talking about?'

Richard strode to the back window, then to the table with his circuits on it. He mumbled something.

'What?'

He put out his hand, letting it hover for a moment, then snatched up a valve.

'Don't just play with your wireless set . . .'

'I am not playing!' he shouted. 'And it is a television receiver!' He pointed a shaking finger at the cathode ray tube. 'Surplus. From the radar station. It will bring pictures out of the air! Probably be the next century before they come to Yorkshire but I wanted you to – to . . . well, be the first to see them. Oh, I know you think it's a silly game . . .'

The baby cried out in her sleep, then settled. Richard now appeared as shocked by his outburst as Paula was. He looked at her as if he had not seen her since she came in. His eyes softened.

'You look beautiful,' he said. He moved towards her but her look stopped him.

'Tell me,' she said. 'What is it?'

He looked at the floor, then at his hands. They were shaking. 'Someone told me you used to go with her brother. Bob Longman.'

'Yes.'

Richard raised his eyes slowly and looked at her, almost as if he were afraid. 'Did you . . . do it with him?'

'Yes,' Paula said coolly. 'I told you.'

'He was the person . . .?'

'Yes.'

163

Richard turned and walked a couple of steps, as if the pain of knowing could be physically avoided. He looked at Paula again. 'Do you write to him?'

'No. What is all this?'

'He writes to you, doesn't he?'

'I'm not answering any more questions!'

Richard came forward quickly and caught her wrist. She looked at him, shocked as his grip tightened.

'Richard!'

She pulled away. He looked at the mark he had made on her wrist, then he turned from her and swept loose parts of his television receiver on to the floor. Paula moved to pick them up.

'Leave them!' he shouted.

She stared at him, paused, then picked up the pieces anyway.

'I can't stop him writing, can I?' she said.

'What do you do with his letters?'

She stood up and put the parts carefully back on the table. Her face was expressionless. 'I throw them away.'

'I expected,' Richard said, his voice wavering, 'I thought, once we got married . . . once we . . . things would change . . .'

'Oh, Richard.' Paula could not withstand the pain on his face. She went to him, putting her hands on his arms, looking squarely into his eyes. 'Richard, I wouldn't hurt you for all –'

'I don't mind being hurt! I just don't . . . want to be your . . . friend!' Every word left his mouth with a jolt of pain. Paula's arms had slipped around him. They held each other. 'Is she mine?'

'Of course she is,' Paula said against his shoulder.

He became very still, his arms dropping away from her. Paula moved back and he turned away to the small table. Something in him was spent, leaving him quieter, harder.

Paula stared at him. 'You do believe me?'

Richard nodded absently, rearranging the parts on the table. When he spoke his tone was practical, matter-of-fact. 'You lied about the letters. You kept them.'

That was true. She had lied. Why? Suddenly she couldn't keep still, couldn't look at him. She felt sick. She moved towards the hall, mumbling, barely audible. 'I didn't want to hurt you. You're like the rest.'

'What?' Richard turned. 'What did you say?' Now that it was out he was dogged, following her as she picked up the baby. 'I've got to know the truth, Paula. Is that why your mother threw you out?'

Paula was preparing a reasoned answer but sudden anger flooded through her. 'Yes!' she shouted. 'It is! Yes!'

She turned away, hugging the baby close, sensing rather than seeing Richard go to the small table and sit down, pick up a valve. It was true. That *was* why she had been thrown out. It was surprising how vindictive she felt. If Richard wanted to build something out of that, well, let him! She was fed up of rumours, gossip ...! Wasn't the bitter irony that sometimes, just sometimes, when she went across to Mafeking Park to see Vera she wanted them to be true?

Richard was absorbed now in connecting a wire. Well, if he wanted to think that, as fanciful as his pictures in the air, let him!

18

Bob had never doubted that a time would come when the last prisoner would be processed and the greater part of his job would evaporate. As the weeks and months passed at Neufeld Camp he watched the trends: smaller intake numbers, shorter advance agendas and listings, lower figures pencilled on the semi-classified target graphs kept in Lieutenant Gray's desk. A day came when Bob realized they were soon to finish here. The job was nearly complete.

He mentioned it to Sergeant McCulloch, more in the spirit of thankfulness than with any regret. 'It should be civvy street before we know it,' he added, and immediately saw McCulloch grin.

When the job was finished, he said, they would be moving, not leaving. 'It's a case of last in, last out,' he said. 'You'll recall you were a bit of a latecomer, Longman. They'll be reluctant to lose you. I reckon you'll stay in the Army, in one job or another, for at least another year before they let you go.'

The news, as it settled on Bob, reminded him of a freezing day in France, when they had struggled to the top of a hill, feeling half-dead from exhaustion, only to find there was another hill, just as big, dead ahead of them. Two or three men had actually begun to cry.

Bob felt like that now. Anger threatened to swamp him as he threw things back and forward across his desk, cursing the Army and his own unique brand of luck, clinging to him like a bad smell.

After a whole day of feeling so sickened he couldn't even do the automatic parts of his job correctly, he had a sleepless night shot through with every dark conjecture his imagination could devise. By morning, anger had finally been exhausted. It left an ache of frustration which at least allowed him to do his job.

At the first opportunity he sat down at his desk and painfully composed a letter to Paula, explaining his predicament, and closing by telling her he could not stand her continuing silence, not now that she had given birth to Carol Vera.

He put the letter in the post and got back to his daily round. The difference, now, was that his awareness and ingenuity were readjusted. They were tuned to finding an alternative to serving another whole, unthinkable year in the Army.

On a bright Tuesday morning a car drove slowly along Roberts Avenue, the driver peering out at the house numbers as he passed. Cars rarely came down that street and as this one went by an occasional curtain twitched. Several people were watching as the car stopped outside number 15 and a smart young RAF officer got out. He stood and adjusted his tight collar, flicked something invisible from the front of his jacket, and knocked on the door. Paula opened it.

'Mrs Austen?' He went through the rigmarole of

identifying her as Richard Austen's wife and himself as Flight Lieutenant Pritchard.

They sat opposite each other in the tiny back room. Pritchard composed himself. He had done this kind of thing before, but this was nasty, worse than usual.

Ten hours earlier, he said, on a night flight to test experimental navigational equipment, there had been an engine failure resulting in the plane crashing into a wood twenty miles from base. Richard had been killed.

She said nothing. She was just staring at some half-built radio equipment on the little table by the window. God, this was terrible. He was supposed to have a WAAF with him to handle the emotional stuff, but they were demobbing them at a rate of knots now.

'Was anybody else killed?' she said.

He wasn't supposed to say more but it wasn't fair. She would find out anyway after the inquiry.

'He was alone.'

'He was a radio operator! He didn't fly.'

'He wanted to . . . he'd clocked up some flying hours . . . It was . . . an unofficial flight . . . He just . . . took the aircraft.'

Paula couldn't look at him. She stared at the half-finished television set as Pritchard tried to be kind, but everything he said just made things worse.

'He'd been in a funny mood this last couple of weeks . . . it was almost as if he was back in the war. It was quite out of character . . .'

When Pritchard had gone, Paula put Richard's television set carefully in an Atora Suet box for safe keeping. As she did so there hammered in her head their last conversation. *If that's what he wants to think, let him think it.* He had thought it. This was terrible. Terrible. It was the lie about the letters. The keeping of those letters. Terrible. Terrible. She tore and twisted Bob's letters and burned them in the grate. She beat the ash into small fragments. She sat down and wrote Bob a letter, explaining how she had got rid of his baby ... 'That's what you wanted, why you went off, isn't it ...' and that she had then married a good man, and had his child.

The nearest post box was in Mafeking Park but she made a considerable detour, walked into town and posted it there. She wheeled the baby round for hours until it was dark. Her mother had never seen Carol. For the first time she felt like going back to her old house. She should tell her about Richard. But in the end she couldn't face it. She was exhausted when she got back but couldn't sleep. She swept out the grate obsessively, making sure every fragment of ash was in the bin. It was dawn before she finally fell asleep in a chair.

In Neufeld twelve days later Bob saw the post arrive but took little notice. Vera was the only one who wrote to him, and he'd had a letter last week. He was, in any case, preoccupied. Tomorrow was the day scheduled for B Company's withdrawal from the camp. Bob was a couple of hundred yards away from the admin hut, watching a German prisoner remove a screen panel from a latrine. As the man prepared to fill in the hole Bob stepped forward.

'*Raus!*' he shouted. '*Schnell!*'

The prisoner made no protest. He simply turned and went away. Bob stood for a moment, looking around. Of course he wasn't going to do anything . . . but he couldn't resist finding out if there was anything in Karl von Berner's story . . .

The post at the admin hut was attracting the attention of everyone in the vicinity, Lieutenant Gray and Sergeant McCulloch among them. As Bob stood there, reassuring himself he was not being watched, he heard Karl von Berner's words again: *Small fortune . . . you think it's a fairy story, but I can prove it . . .*

Bob walked with apparent aimlessness across the rough ground near the place where the screen had stood. After a few moments he saw the open end of a rusted, half-buried rain pipe. He looked around again, then bent down swiftly, slipped his fingers inside the pipe and pulled out a ragged bundle held together with an elastic band.

He straightened, turned his back to the activity by the admin hut and looked down. He saw he was holding a thick wad of high-denomination US dollar bills. He riffled the end of the bundle, seeing tens, fifties, hundreds. When he pulled off the band and spread the bundle he saw that every bill was in fact only a half.

He looked up sharply at a sound and saw Karl von Berner, five yards away, watching him.

'Where did you get this from?' Bob demanded.

'I could show you the other half,' von Berner said calmly.

This was a con trick! Obviously! Even if it wasn't, he'd be stupid to get involved.

'Get stuffed!' he shouted. 'You're showing nobody nothing! You lot are moving out!'

Bob thrust the notes into his pocket and marched off towards the admin hut. Von Berner, expressionless, watched him go.

Another lorry arrived as Bob reached the hut. There was bustling activity as boxes filled with papers and equipment were stacked outside the hut. Arthur came across.

'One for you.'

Bob stared at the handwriting. He'd only had one letter from Paula before but he knew every curl, loop, every dashed 't'. His heart pounding, he went round the side of the hut to read it in private. Only Arthur saw him.

Eva drew Arthur aside. 'You're going?' she said.

Arthur was too preoccupied to answer. He was watching Bob, who looked as if he had been shot.

'Is it from Paula?' Arthur said.

Bob did not reply. He turned suddenly and marched into the hut.

Inside, Lieutenant Gray and another officer were talking on the telephones. Two soldiers were filling packing cases. Bob stood near his empty desk, stricken, hearing the words of the letter repeat themselves over and over in his head.

'Don't just stand there, Longman,' Sergeant McCulloch said, appearing behind him. 'Move it!'

Bob did not respond. Lieutenant Gray put down the

telephone as McCulloch dropped a bundle of forms on the desk in front of him.

'They're not complete, sir,' McCulloch said.

Gray scowled at him. 'We can't transport prisoners without documentation, Sergeant McCulloch.'

'I'm a bit short-handed, sir.' He threw a meaningful look at Bob.

'Longman,' Gray said, picking up the telephone again, 'give him a hand.'

Bob turned mechanically and moved towards the stacked papers. For the remainder of the morning he worked steadily, moving files, sorting documents and packing boxes. In the afternoon he helped load boxes and crates on to lorries, until hardly a trace remained of the British Army's presence in Neufeld Camp. Throughout the long day he worked in silence, like an automaton, containing his shock, bottling it until it began to dissipate and diffuse, becoming something else inside him.

In the early evening he saw Arthur by the main gate. He looked thoroughly miserable.

'Has she gone?' Bob said. 'Eva?'

Arthur nodded.

'What happened?'

'Nothing,' Arthur said. 'I think she's right nice. The nicest . . .' his voice broke and he shook his head. He looked at Bob, openly suffering. 'It was awful. She was so angry. She invited me to supper. She didn't seem to understand why I couldn't go.'

Bob could scarcely believe him. 'On our last night? And you said no?'

'We're not allowed in German homes,' Arthur protested.

'Not allowed?' Bob glared at him. 'Oh, dear. You spineless bugger. You'll never get nowhere, Arthur, if you don't take what's not allowed.'

He gripped Arthur by the arm and led him towards the billets. It was a long time since Arthur had seen Bob like this – not since he had been made up to a Corporal. He had sworn never to get involved in any stupid escapades again. But the thought of Eva's angry look . . . and even more, the thought of never seeing her again . . .

'I'll take you,' Bob said. 'I've got a pass into town. I'll wangle you one. You're only going for a drink, aren't you!'

'Well . . . just a drink, then . . .'

A short time after, as Bob stood combing his hair, peering into a scrap of mirror propped on his desk, he looked up and saw McCulloch watching him. After a few final sweeps at the sides, Bob pocketed the comb.

'See you later, Sarge,' he said cheerily, heading for the door.

McCulloch nodded. 'I'm having an early night,' he said.

When Bob had gone McCulloch switched out the light, opened the hut door and stood back in the shadows, watching. He saw Bob climb into a jeep. Another soldier came along the side of the vehicle and got in beside Bob. For a brief moment, but long enough to be recognized, Arthur's face appeared in the light before Bob threw the engine into gear and drove off.

McCulloch went back into the office. Most of the files had gone, but a few index boxes were still there. He opened one and flipped through the cards until he found what he wanted. He pulled out the card and looked at it under the light: NOLTE, Eva, Waldstrasse 17.

19

After a series of wrong turns and several minutes of doubling back, Bob finally swung the jeep into the end of Waldstrasse and stopped. The street was deserted. There was no other traffic and nothing was parked. The only hints of life were occasional chinks of light at the sides of windows.

Bob switched off the engine. He picked up a beer bottle and unscrewed the cap, the sound of it abnormally loud on the silent street. There was less than a third of the bottle left. He threw back his head and began drinking it.

'Let's go,' Arthur said.

Bob choked and spluttered as the beer went down the wrong way. He wiped his mouth with the back of his hand and blinked at Arthur. 'Go?'

'She's probably in bed,' Arthur said.

'Exactly.' Bob grinned. 'Lovely and warm.'

Arthur looked openly alarmed. Bob pushed him and he got out of the jeep. On the pavement he bent over and peered in. 'What are you going to do?' he asked.

'Get pissed,' Bob told him. 'Back in an hour.'

Arthur turned away, then came back. 'What number was it?'

'*Siebzehn*. Seventeen.'

Arthur nodded and walked away again. Bob started the engine and Arthur came running back, waving his arms. 'Wait!' he said. 'She might not be in!'

Bob pointed and Arthur turned. The door of number 17 had been partly opened. When Eva saw Arthur she opened it fully and stepped into the street.

'I knew you'd come,' she said, smiling.

It occurred to Bob, with an impact something like a punch, that the last thing he wanted to see at the present moment was the way Arthur and Eva were looking at each other. He jerked the engine into gear.

'I'll come back,' he said.

'Don't be stupid,' Arthur said, and looked at Eva for support.

'Bob must come too,' she said.

She had been getting ready for bed. Her outdoor coat was slung over her partially unbuttoned dress. A glimpse of her breasts was not helping matters.

'No thanks,' he said. 'I'm going for a drink.' He needed several! He was going to get absolutely blind.

'I have a bottle I was saving,' Eva said, in immense high spirits that Arthur had turned up after all. 'I was just beginning to think I would have to drink it myself.'

She turned and showed Arthur into the house. Reluctantly Bob switched off the engine and followed them.

It took ten minutes for him to start regretting he had come. There was beer and a bottle of fine schnapps, and Eva did her best to make him feel welcome, but Arthur's doting, calf-eyed attention to her was more than he could stand. He kept feeling

Paula's letter in his pocket. Once he went to the lavatory, reading it, as if the words could have changed or somehow he had got the wrong meaning.

He soon drank all the beer and most of the schnapps, finally withdrawing with his glass to a chair in the corner, where he sat staring into space while Arthur and Eva giggled and whispered together.

He ought to go. Leave them to it. But they were just having a laugh, a giggle, a fondle – Arthur looked as if he'd never get round to it! In the circumstances, for Bob, it was an exquisite kind of torture. Now they were pissing around making ersatz barley coffee in the kitchen. Why didn't he just take her upstairs and shag her?

Arthur came in from the kitchen, carrying three cups.

'You've got half an hour,' Bob told him.

Arthur put down the cups, his smile fading. He began to look panicky.

Bob pointed at the door. 'I'll wait outside.'

'You can't do that!'

'Well, I'm not going to stay and watch!' Bob swayed, steadied himself and moved to the door.

'There's nothing to watch . . .'

'Just knock her off and get it done with.'

'I don't want to just knock her off!' Arthur waved his arm helplessly. 'Not like this!'

Bob came back. 'What the hell do you mean? There's only one way to do it.'

Eva came in with the coffee. 'To do what?' she said.

Bob turned to her. It was some trick of the light, or

177

more likely the fatal combination of beer and schnapps, but somehow her face was more like Paula's than ever. He blinked and refocused. What was he on about? She was nothing like her.

'To do what?' Eva was repeating.

'One way to make love,' he said flatly.

'Come on, Bob.' Was this Arthur yacking away? He was unimportant, because Eva had become Paula again. He wanted to talk to her about her letter, but he had to carry on with this stupid conversation.

'I was just giving Arthur a few tips,' he slurred.

Eva frowned. 'Tips?'

'Shut up, will you,' Arthur said.

'Lessons,' Bob said carefully, as if he were addressing a child.

Eva moved towards Arthur, her look serious now, protective. 'I do not think he needs those,' she said.

'Oh, he does,' Bob said, grinning lopsidedly. 'I had to start him off, didn't I? With the vink.'

Eva laughed uneasily. She was Eva again, but she had something to do with Paula, the letter, he couldn't work it out. She was giving him the come-on anyway, that was certain.

'In at the start, so I have to be in at the finish,' Bob said. 'Don't I?' He stepped back, standing up straight, impersonating a parade-ground McCulloch. He extended his arm sharply, pointing at Eva. 'Hidentify the parts of this deadly weapon, Spence. That's an order.'

'Come on,' Arthur said flatly. 'Let's go.'

'Please don't go, Arthur,' Eva pleaded.

'I'll give you a hand, as it were,' Bob said, continuing

his best McCulloch impersonation. He began pointing to parts of Eva, almost touching her. 'Hair. Vinks. Lips. Er . . .'

He stopped at her breasts, putting a look of comical confusion on his face. Arthur looked at the floor.

'Breakdown of weapon,' Bob said. 'By numbers – comm . . . ence . . . now! One! The vink! Come on Spence! Two! The touch!' He touched Eva and she giggled. 'Three!' He leaned forward and kissed her on the mouth.

Eva pushed him away. Well, he knew that one. They always did that hard-to-get stuff. He looked at her for a second, then he pushed her back, hard. They loved it really. Arthur grabbed him and Bob slammed him against the wall.

'Stop it!' Eva screamed. 'Stop it!'

'Come on,' Bob shouted. He'd had enough of this playing around. 'He doesn't want you and I've done all this fucking work . . .'

He grabbed her but she hit him, slipping from his grasp, moving aside every time he reached for her. He punched the table suddenly, scaring her badly, and in the moment she froze he grabbed her by the shoulders and began shouting in her face.

'Bitch! You're like her, you're one thing then another, you're all the same, you bitch!' He took a step back, his hands coming away from her shoulders. 'Four!' His fingers hooked in the top of Eva's dress and ripped it downwards, exposing her breasts.

He was out of control then. He hadn't had anything for so long. He was on her, his hand in the warmth of

179

her as Arthur started hammering blows on his head and shoulders. They fought, stumbling and rolling, kicking over a chair, upsetting the table, making so much noise they didn't hear the banging on the door. As it got louder and more insistent Eva ran upstairs. Bob punched Arthur on the mouth and ran after her.

The door burst open and Sergeant McCulloch ran in, followed by two Redcaps. Bob, half-way up the stairs, saw them and stopped where he was. He stared at them across the shambles of the room, seeing the triumph in McCulloch's eye. He looked happier than he'd been for months as Bob hung his head and let his hands droop at his sides. Nothing mattered. They could do anything they liked with him, anything at all.

Shortly before midnight Bob was brought before Lieutenant Gray in the office of the admin hut at Neufeld Camp. Gray had dressed hurriedly, omitting the tie, and his hair stood up in irregular spikes. He sat behind his desk staring at Bob, seeing the bruises on his face and his cut hands. The handcuffs had been clamped over a graze on one of his wrists and now it looked raw and angry.

Gray listened to the summary of events from Sergeant McCulloch, then dismissed him and the Redcaps. He said nothing to Bob until the door closed behind them. Bob stared at the bare wall behind Gray's chair, his face blank.

'You're lucky she's refusing to say anything,' Gray told him. 'But a brawl over a German woman, in her house, is bad enough. You've let me down.'

'I'm sorry.'

'You've let yourself down, man!'

Bob shrugged, implying the damage to his integrity was of no consequence. Gray looked harder at him, sensing the despair.

'What happened? I don't mean tonight. What did she write to you?'

Bob looked at the Lieutenant but his eyes were unfocused. 'Permission to go, sir, please. Or be locked up. Whatever.'

'Tell me,' Gray insisted.

Bob stared past him. His throat moved, then he began to speak in a mumble. 'She doesn't want me to see her again or to write to her.'

Gray had begun to compose a platitude to cover the situation, but abandoned it when Bob continued.

'The child isn't mine, sir. She killed him.'

The pain in Bob's voice was so raw, so stark, that Gray looked away for a moment.

'I thought of him as Tony, sir, after you . . .'

For a moment Gray feared the naked emotion was sinking into counterfeit sentiment. He looked at Bob again and saw he was wrong. Every word was true, every feeling.

'I was a father, don't you see, sir, a lot of men they're not very interested, I used to jeer at it, but I suppose it's bringing up our two youngest, and somehow over these few months I've lived with him, with him and her and . . . and . . . and . . .' He blinked hard and stared at Lieutenant Gray. 'What right had she to kill him, sir? Tell me, tell me! What right? What right?'

'Steady, steady – calm down!'

'What's the point of calming down?' Bob yelled. 'I'll kill her!'

'Oh don't be stupid!'

Gray looked into Bob's eyes and saw something repellently cold. It was such a change, and so sudden in its appearance, that Gray forgot what he was going to say next. When Bob spoke, his voice had turned flat, the tone humdrum.

'That's what my father did,' he said. 'Killed the woman he was living with. They would have topped him if he hadn't died in prison. It runs in the family.'

Gray was mesmerized, momentarily, by the cool, prosaic way Bob said that. He sat up sharply and reminded himself of his authority. He struggled to make his voice sharper, more whiplike.

'I should have you locked up now. But we're short of men. You've organized your trucks. You're ... bloody efficient and I need you. You'll be charged at your next post.'

'Yes, sir.'

'I trust you,' Gray said, 'God knows why. I want you to get there tomorrow, without fail, on time and without doing anything stupid. And I want your word on that.'

'You have my word, sir.'

'Go on. Get out and get some sleep.'

'Thank you, sir.'

Bob saluted and went out.

20

The big move began early next morning. Details of prisoners' identities and their status particulars were checked against War Department transit lists, after which they were shepherded into trucks. Bob supervised the trucks for which he had responsibility, moving from one to the other, acting as no more than a supervisory presence now that the hard work had been done. At one full truck Arthur Spence was making a head count of prisoners before the grille was put on the back. Bob glanced over Arthur's shoulder at his list. They did not look directly at each other.

'Arthur, listen,' Bob said, 'I –'

'Piss off.'

Was it at that moment he decided? Arthur walked away to where another group of prisoners were waiting to be checked. Bob went the opposite way, approaching an empty truck with prisoners gathered at the back. He saw one of them was Karl von Berner. Their eyes met for a fraction of a second. It was a signal, an agreement. From that moment onwards he was on a course he couldn't stop. Bob glanced aside at a prisoner everyone knew by his first name – Hermann, perennially sour, a man who never seemed to stop complaining. This morning his face was particularly strained as he grumbled to one of the guards.

'What's the matter?' Bob asked von Berner.

Von Berner shrugged. He turned to Hermann. '*Was ist los? Sind sie krank?*'

Hermann clutched his stomach. '*Ich fühle mich nicht wohl. Ich brauche einen Arzt. Jetzt!*'

'He wants a doctor,' von Berner said. 'His stomach – if he could have some water it will help.'

Bob told the guard to get water for Hermann. During these brief exchanges Hermann was obviously struggling to understand what was being said. Von Berner explained to him, and Hermann started to complain louder. They had a spirited altercation which von Berner ended abruptly by holding up a stiff, warning finger.

'*Ruhe! Horen sie mir?*'

Hermann went quiet, but his lips still moved and he went on rubbing his stomach. Bob felt no apprehension. No fear.

All he had to do was make sure Hermann and von Berner were in the same truck.

Within the hour the first convoy of three trucks and their escort vehicles had moved off. Bob's transport was in the centre of the column behind one of the trucks. He sat beside the driver, chewing gum, never once looking back at Neufeld Camp. They drove at a steady speed through variable countryside, passing dense woods and broad sunny hillsides, easing steadily north along roads pitted and rubble-strewn from German and Allied shelling.

After a while there was a commotion in the truck directly ahead. Some prisoners came to the grille and shouted. Bob stuck his head out of the window to hear. He was not surprised to find that the trouble was Hermann.

'He needs a doctor,' one of the prisoners shouted.

Bob glanced ahead. They were approaching the perimeter of a very densely wooded area.

'Wait until we're through the forest,' he called back.

He sat back and went on chewing. Von Berner looked through the grille. Bob didn't meet his eyes. The convoy ploughed on into the heart of the forest, the branches above so thickly interlaced it was hard to believe it was still daylight. Bob saw a prisoner hammering on the grille with both hands, and he could see others banging on the sides of the truck. He stuck his head out of the window again.

'He's very bad!' the prisoner yelled, 'and he's stinking us out!'

Bob muttered to his driver, who sounded the horn three times. The convoy slowed down and came to a halt. As the engines died and the drumming stopped, the silence of the forest quickly closed in. Soldiers jumped from the escort vehicles, rifles ready, keeping close to the trucks for cover. It was a regular drill and everyone was alert to any possibility of trouble. Bob got out of his vehicle, looked around carefully, then went in search of a medic.

The first response to possible danger having passed, soldiers began to relax. Rifles were lowered and cigarettes were lit. Prisoners stared out from the gloom of their trucks at the dark green canopy overhead.

Bob returned with a medic and stood waiting as

soldiers with rifles surrounded the back of the truck while the grille was opened. The medic climbed on to the metal step and prepared to squeeze into the truck to examine Hermann. Soldiers waved their rifles and shouted at the prisoners in the truck to move back.

In the moment between the gap in the grille opening to its widest and the medic blocking the space with his body, Karl von Berner pushed through the space, colliding with the medic and knocking him aside. For another second the medic's body formed a shield between the German and the soldiers on the ground.

Bob was the first to fire. He had the temptation to hit von Berner. For a fleeting moment he could have done so. But von Berner vanished into the forest, moments before the rifles began firing.

Bob ran after him, calling to two soldiers, Midge and Geoff, to follow him. They went crashing through the undergrowth, hearing von Berner ahead of them, his thrashing movements like a delayed echo of their own. Bob kept a fix on the German, listening hard, gesturing wildly for Geoff and Midge to fan out. As they moved away from him he plunged through a thicket of trees and bushes, hearing them diminish behind him, their sounds absorbed by the trees. He could still hear von Berner, though, and he kept on running, his pistol cocked and ready.

Without warning, as von Berner had told him, the forest suddenly began to clear. So much was true, at least. Bob was running on a path with tractor marks along either side. He stopped and looked around. Ahead was a wide clearing with tidy piles of chopped wood. There was no one in sight and it was perfectly quiet. He breathed carefully, listening, turning his head in a slow circle. If von Berner had lied to him about the money he would shoot him. After all, he was an escaping prisoner.

A sudden clatter of birds overhead made him jump and spin round. He turned at another sound on his left and found himself looking straight at Karl von Berner, standing three feet away. In the moment it took Bob to bring up his gun, von Berner hit him savagely on the head with a length of wood. The cracking sound of it echoed briefly across the clearing as Bob fell face down in the dirt.

Hardship had never touched Paula's life before. In the past, being hard-up meant there were annoying shortages of funds, minor limitations on spending that were neither distressing nor permanent. Now, trying to live on the hopeless pittance the government gave her, watching her small reserves of cash dwindle day by day, she was forced into contact with a level of misery she could never have imagined. Money, she discovered, was practically everything, since little was possible when you had none. Nothing else had a fraction of money's power; it had no substitute, and there was no consolation for being without it.

Paula's standards, inevitably, were collapsing. She was quite often untidy in her dress, even dishevelled, and she went out on the street looking that way, lacking any incentive to make herself presentable. Her clothes were wearing out; odd sums she might have spent on things to improve her life in small ways, she spent on Carol instead.

Amazingly, it seemed to affect her looks, her hair, her skin, until she looked like where she came from – Mafeking Park. She knew the cause of it, too: it was the absence from her life – and theirs – of hope and colour. Money could reverse all that. Money, at a more mundane and urgent level, could pay the rent so a woman could sleep at night instead of fretting about being evicted if she missed one more week.

She found it was nearly impossible to get a job. Suddenly, where they had been crying out for women to work in factories, now they did not want them. One morning she saw Fred Spence standing on a corner with his snap tin under his arm, waiting for his lift to work in a Winter's Engineering lorry. She went across and asked him, right out and without preamble, if he could put in a word for her at the factory. He shook his head, and she could tell he would rather not have had this encounter.

'It's all heavy engineering now,' he said.

'That's what I did!' She reminded him that during the war she had been a welder. That might be so, Fred countered, but men were coming home. It wouldn't be right for women to take their jobs.

'Mine isn't coming home,' she told him bluntly. 'I'll take his job.'

'I'm sorry, Paula . . .' Fred moved to the edge of the pavement as his lift approached. 'The war's over. All workers now have to be members of the Engineering Union.'

'I'll join.'

'They've only just started taking women members, love. Let them get used to it.' And that was that.

It was the baby, alone, who gave Paula's life what warmth and sense of direction it possessed, allowed her to think of the future.

Most of the dreams about the future in Mafeking Park took place in the Blue Anchor. It would all be so much better, Sal Longman said, when her Bob got back and threw himself into all the opportunities waiting to be taken by bright lads like him.

'Have you heard from him?' Sue asked her.

Sal was talking to Dick Moxham and Sue, with Miss Thwaites chiming in. Sal said she had not heard from Bob recently.

'It's the last lap that's worst, isn't it?' Miss Thwaites sighed. This was the kind of comfort Sal did not want to hear.

'Oh, I'd know if there was anything wrong,' Sal said, flattening a red hand over her left breast. 'I love them all, but our Bob's special. If anything happened to him I'd feel it here.'

'Like twins do,' Miss Thwaites said.

'Aye,' Sal said, missing the sarcasm. 'Well, you only hurt the one you love, Sue. You know that.' Sal sniffed loudly, the maudlin turn of mood threatening to overwhelm her. 'That was the time I had my little problem.' She stared down into her glass. 'I said Bob, I said, you're needed. I can handle my own little Hitler.'

She drained the glass and slapped it down on the counter. Sue put it under the pump for a refill. As she began to pull the handle Sal put up her hand.

'You know what?' she said. 'I'm not going to have another until he gets back.'

Sue clung to the pump, not sure if she was serious. Sal made an elaborate gesture of rejection towards the glass.

'I mean it. My war effort . . .'

'It's over,' Miss Thwaites said, rolling her eyes. 'Haven't you heard?'

Sal shook her head firmly. 'It's over for me when my Bob gets back.'

The forest was so serene and peaceful that it would have been hard to imagine a full-scale manhunt in such a setting. It had been three weeks since the escape of the German prisoner, and the woodsman who worked in the clearing at the centre of the forest had been told they never caught him. The woodsman did not know whether to be pleased about that, or sorry. If a German soldier had run away from his captors because he was sick to be back with his family and his heart would break if he did not see them soon, well that was one thing. If some murdering Nazi bastard had escaped the clutches of justice, that was another thing entirely. What mattered, in the long run, was that the soldiers, German and British, no longer came this way in large numbers, and the woodsman could carry on his job without being hampered.

On this warm sunny morning the woodsman's six-year-old grandson, Max, was stalking prey – his cousin Erich – through the underbrush around the clearing. Max had not made up his mind yet where it would be best to look. He was enjoying the stealth too much, the way he could creep through sun-dappled, dew-bright leaves with deep shadows underneath, where he could duck down and become invisible in a moment.

A fly buzzed at Max's ear and he swatted it. He stood still and listened. He could hear more flies, buzzing like bees, not far off. Flies clung near people; he had seen them buzz around his grandfather while he worked, so why shouldn't they gather around Erich? Max let out an animal cry, then moved off at a crouch towards the buzzing.

Peering through the long grass, he saw a patch of clothing, like Erich's jacket, jutting up from the shrubbery several feet away. Flies seemed to be buzzing over it in large numbers. Max grinned at the thrill of finding his prey so quickly, so stealthily. He moved closer, working his way past shrubs and tiny bushes, keeping his eye on the cloth, which looked now like an elbow sticking up.

A fly boomed near his ear. He shook his head to drive it off. He crouched again, watching the prey, the dark brown cloth, then with a cry of triumph he dashed forward and landed on it with outstretched hands.

The cry cut off in his throat. It turned to a piercing scream as Max backed away, terrified, wiping and wiping his hands on the wet grass.

A few yards away Erich came out of his hiding place and looked. He saw the flies re-gathering above the spot Max had run from. He moved closer and saw an arm in a sleeve with two stripes, and above the arm the black, swollen remains of something that looked like a man's face.

Two hours later Arthur Spence was driving Second Lieutenant Gray through the forest in a jeep when they saw a group of British Military Policemen standing huddled in a clearing. Gray told Arthur to stop. They got out and approached. One of the men who was smoking nipped out the cigarette as they came near. Gray and Arthur wrinkled their noses in unison when they caught the smell from the body. As soon as Arthur saw it, spreadeagled in the grass, he looked away.

One of the Redcaps, a Sergeant, explained that a child had found the body, and that the grandfather had alerted the nearest military security unit.

Gray got down and looked at it. It was face down, with a clear bullet-hole in the back of the head. The face was unrecognizable, bloated and half eaten by rats. The hair had gone. Leaking fluids of putrefaction had stained and darkened the uniform, but it was still clearly that of a corporal in the North Yorkshires.

'Any ID?' Gray asked.

One of the MPs passed him an identity tag. Gray looked at it, passed it to Arthur. He turned it in the sunlight: CORPORAL ROBERT LONGMAN.

'Anything else?' Gray said.

The MP handed him an envelope. Gray opened it. There was a folded newspaper clipping he had seen before, and other papers, Paula's last letter to Bob among them.

Arthur walked away into the forest, fumbling for a cigarette. Gray left him to himself for a few minutes, before going to speak to him.

That evening, as a military clerk finished gathering up the end-of-day papers from Lieutenant Gray's desk, saluted the Lieutenant and left the office, Sergeant McCulloch entered. He had been waiting for the soldier to go. He saluted the Lieutenant, who had Bob's ID tag and the envelope with his papers on the desk in front of him.

McCulloch nodded to the report on the desk. 'It's pretty obvious, sir.'

'What is obvious, Sergeant McCulloch?'

'Longman set up von Berner's escape and then –'

'Why would he do anything as stupid as that?'

'He was in the shit,' McCulloch said. 'Von Berner tried his hidden treasure malarkey on others –'

'That's the rumour, is it?' Gray got to his feet. He put his hands flat on the desk. 'You've not a shred of evidence! Longman went after the escaping prisoner and was killed by him or by some other fanatic. *That's* obvious. Anyway, there's no point in pursuing it.'

Gray sat down again. McCulloch remained where he was, silently demanding attention.

'What is it?' Gray said.

'Permission to point out that I recommended Corporal Longman be removed from the escort, sir.'

'Thank you for reminding me, Sergeant,' Gray said coldly. 'But it's in the report.'

21

Mrs Wickham let Jack out of the house ahead of her, then she locked the front door and walked behind him to his Austin Ten, parked by the kerb. Half-way along the path she stopped.

'No, Jack,' she said, shaking her head, 'I can't do it.'

'Come on, Sarah!' For once Jack wasn't laughing. He unlocked the car door. 'You've got to go!'

'I've written to her. Has she replied?' She glanced aside, picturing her own affront. 'I know what will happen. She said I'd never understand and she's right about that, if nothing else.' She turned back towards the house. 'Words would stick in my throat if I ever clapped eyes on her again.'

The street lights began to come on, all down the street.

'My God!' Mrs Wickham put a hand to her chest. 'My heart. I can't get used to it, you know. Lights. Just having lights.'

They stood together for a minute like children in a fairy tale. Soon the whole length of the street was lit.

Jack turned to the car. 'Come on, Sarah,' he said quietly, opening the door.

In the upstairs bedroom at number 15 Roberts Avenue, Carol had finally gone to sleep. It had been one of the evenings when, in spite of all reason, Paula had begun to believe the child might never sleep again. In the end the descent into slumber had been fitful and twitchy, and now although her breathing had steadied, Carol's eyelids still moved, threatening – or so Paula imagined – to fly wide open again at any second, the prelude to a bout of prolonged howling.

As Paula stood up and gazed at the little face, car headlights passed across her sleeping features, producing the tiniest wince. She slept on.

Paula clasped her hands in a prayer of thanks as she tiptoed from the room. When she was half-way down the stairs, stepping with care to avoid the creaky parts, the doorbell rang. She stiffened for a split second, shocked. Then she dashed forward, banging her knee in her panic to get to the door before the bell rang again. With fire flaring across her kneecap she wrenched open the door, a finger ready at her lips, her other hand rubbing her knee. She found herself looking at Uncle Jack.

'Hello, Paula.'

'Ssh! Hello.'

Jack stared at her as Mrs Wickham emerged from the shadows behind him. Paula saw her and forgot her knee. She pulled the door shut a little, so they would not see the chaos inside.

'I'm sorry about Richard,' her mother said.

Paula nodded. 'I got your letter. Thank you.'

'Mrs Winter phoned up with her condolences,' Mrs Wickham explained stiffly. 'She read it in the paper. I had to pretend I knew.' She paused, hands folded, staring at Paula. 'Well? Are you going to let us in, or are we just going to stand here?'

In the back room Jack did his best to look at ease. Paula said she would make tea and scurried off to the kitchen. Mrs Wickham stood just inside the door, surveying the room in a dumbfounded silence. She took in the thin rug, the flimsy cheap furniture, the dust on the mantelpiece and table.

Paula brought in a tray with three cups of tea, one of them black. Mrs Wickham stared at that one as Paula put down the tray on the table.

'What is that?'

'I don't take milk,' Paula said. In fact there had barely been enough for one cup.

'First I've heard of it,' Mrs Wickham said. She sat down with her cup, doing it gingerly as if the chair might collapse under her. 'Where's the clock we bought you?'

'I'm having it repaired.'

The momentary silence was as eloquent as a rebuke. Jack peered at a citation to Richard in a frame at one end of the mantelpiece.

'Grateful country,' he muttered. 'They don't give you much more than gratitude, do they?'

Paula was staring at the box with Richard's embryo television set, her hand gripped around the undrinkable cup of tea. Beneath the stiff calm of her face she was at screaming point. She had coped with another misery of a day, aiming herself towards this blissful period, this time that should have been a small oasis of peace, and instead she had this to cope with . . .

'I'll manage,' she said, responding to Jack's remark.

'Well, you don't have to,' Mrs Wickham announced. 'Mrs Winter said she'd be glad to have you back now things are returning to normal.'

'Normal?' Paula glared at her mother. 'Things are not going back to *normal*! I'm not a servant!'

'You'd be better off if you were!'

'Here,' Jack said, getting between them, 'Come on . . .'

'You keep out of this, Jack.' Mrs Wickham glared accusingly at Paula. 'He saw the clock in a second-hand shop.'

Paula blinked, a slow down and up movement of her eyelids that seemed to brush aside her mother's outrage. 'I didn't get much for it. Westminster chimes? It was foreign. Cheap.' She watched her mother's eyes waver. 'I'll get a job. I'll manage. Don't worry about me.'

Mrs Wickham looked up at the ceiling. 'It's not you we're worried about.'

Paula threw her a look of unvarnished hate. 'She's perfectly all right, thank you, mother.'

Mrs Wickham started to rise, then put her hand to her heart. Jack moved towards her, visibly concerned.

'She's all right,' Paula said.

Mrs Wickham pushed herself to her feet, her face churning. 'The baby's all right,' she snapped. 'I'm all right. You're all right. Everything's all right. Good! That's that. Nobody can say I've not done my duty. Come on, Jack.'

She went to the door.

'That's what you're *really* worried about, isn't it?' Paula yelled after her. 'What people think!'

The knife-point accuracy brought Mrs Wickham round, livid, her mouth cranking open to respond. At that moment the baby began crying, woken by the raised voices.

'Bloody hell!' Paula screamed. It was a real full blooded Mafeking Park scream that made her mother wince. 'Bloody hell! Bloody hell!'

She ran upstairs, lifted the frightened baby and held her close. For a moment she could only stand there, shaking, feeling Carol cry against her neck. There was a sound downstairs, the front door closing. Paula whispered to the baby, rocked her, walked out on to the tiny landing and began walking back and forward with her.

'So that's what all the fuss is about,' Mrs Wickham said. She had seen the baby as she was about to leave and had returned.

She was half-way up the stairs, and at the sound of her voice the baby twisted round and stared down, silenced by her own curiosity. Encouraged by that, Mrs Wickham climbed the remaining stairs. Her customary battery of jewellery glittered in the light, holding the child's eyes.

'We haven't been introduced . . .'

The baby put out a hand to Mrs Wickham. In reality it was her brooch, brightly winking and dazzling, that Carol wanted to touch. The tiny fingers, in the bobbing movement between Paula and Mrs Wickham, finally touched her grandmother's cheek and grasped the flesh. The contact delighted Mrs Wickham.

'. . . But I think you know who I am, don't you?'

In the hallway Jack listened to the tentative sounds above, surmising that the baby had brought about a truce, however frail. He went to the back room, gathered up the tea-cups and took them through to the kitchen. He put them down by the empty milk bottle, then paused. He looked at the heel of bread on the board, a tiny piece of cheese in the gauze-faced food cupboard. Apart from that there was a packet of suet, some flour and an almost empty tin of tea. The signs of lone struggle touched him to the heart, angering him suddenly.

He marched out of the kitchen. Paula was sitting at the foot of the stairs, looking half asleep. Mrs Wickham stood beside her, holding Carol, who was fingering the bright brooch at her throat.

'Get some night things,' Jack told Paula.

The women both stared at him. Their mouths opened to speak at the same time.

'Shut up,' Jack snapped. 'Both of you. I've had enough of both of you.' As Paula stood up he put his arm around her. 'Come on . . .'

His kindness and the physical contact, the first in such a long time, overwhelmed Paula. She stood looking into the back room, bewildered, helpless.

'The place is such a mess . . .'

'We'll sort all that later,' Jack said. 'Come on. Don't say anything, Sarah.'

In the morning Paula woke up to the sound of her

mother opening the bedroom curtains. She struggled to sit up, immediately looking for the baby.

'She's been fed,' Mrs Wickham said. 'She's asleep.'

Through the window Paula could see the place where the air raid shelter had been. Flowers were growing on the spot. It was as if the shelter had never existed. A tray rattled at her elbow and she looked down. It was covered with a snowy white cloth, on which lay a rolled napkin in a silver ring, a cup of tea and a boiled egg in a china egg-cup.

'Non-dried,' Mrs Wickham said, nodding at the egg. 'I got it from under the counter.' As she spoke, tears began to roll down Paula's face. 'What on earth are you crying for now?'

'I don't know.'

'Well, save them for when you do.'

She wanted everything to come out, everything. She wanted to get rid of it, every fragment of it, as she had got rid of his letters, burnt them and then got rid of every flake of ash.

'She *is* Richard's. Those letters, those money orders, they were because ... because, because I was having a child by him and I got rid of it and –' She brushed tears from the side of her mouth. 'Throw me out again. You must throw me out. I seem to kill everything ... destroy ... Throw me out, please ...'

Her collapse into complete distress frightened Mrs Wickham. Passion was alien to that house. She fussed by the bed, trying to calm Paula, and impulsively she flung her arms about her. Paula clung on, like a child, sobbing against the front of her mother's apron.

Later that week, while Paula sat in the garden with Carol, Mrs Wickham and Uncle Jack drove over to Roberts Avenue. Between them they put the bulk of Paula's clothing and the baby's into two suitcases. When they came out to take the bags to the car, Mr Thrush the rent collector had appeared. He stood by the door, book in hand, Homburg square on his head and cycle clips in position. Nodding politely, he waited until they came back from the car.

'She owes two weeks' rent,' he said.

Mrs Wickham looked shocked. 'Are you sure?'

'It's in the book,' said Mr Thrush, investing the words with the solemnity of holy writ. He turned the pages and looked down the column of names and payments. 'Nineteen shillings and sixpence,' he said.

'Nineteen shillings and sixpence,' Mrs Wickham repeated, her voice faint with shock, as if all Paula's other sins paled to nothing beside this lapse.

'Plus,' said Mr Thrush, 'nine shillings and ninepence due tomorrow.'

Mrs Wickham looked almost faint. 'Twenty-nine shillings and threepence,' she said.

With the merest trace of humour, Mr Thrush said, 'I cannot fault your mental arithmetic, madam.'

Down the street, a totter's horse and cart were drawn up. The cart was piled with broken furniture, pots and pans and an assortment of discarded, worn-out household fittings. The totter, sitting stooped on the plank seat behind the horse, had seen the cases being taken from number 15 to the car. He was now clearly watching developments with an eye to possible trade.

Mrs Wickham did not want to stand on the street discussing Paula's arrears. She went inside, followed by Jack and Mr Thrush. In the back room Jack began packing the remainder of Paula's things into cardboard boxes.

'Is the lady keeping the property?' Mr Thrush inquired delicately.

'We're just collecting a few clothes,' Jack said, looking to Mrs Wickham to finish the explanation.

'She's ill,' Mrs Wickham said. 'After the bereavement.' She turned to Jack. 'I mean, she's back with me, isn't she?'

Jack nodded. 'She said she'd think about it.'

Mrs Wickham took up the nodding. 'Think. Aye. She'll think about everything but twenty-nine shillings and threepence.'

Mr Thrush smiled at that.

'I'll talk to her,' Mrs Wickham said.

Jack had finished packing and they turned to go.

'Only,' Mr Thrush said, 'with the men coming home I could fill this five hundred times over.'

They walked to the front door and back out on to the street, Jack leading, carrying the cardboard box. On the pavement, watching Mrs Wickham lock the door, Mr Thrush made a show of tussling with his conscience.

'I'll tell you what,' he said, moving closer with his book, so the red and black figures danced before Mrs Wickham's eyes. 'Let me have the keys now and I might be able to forget this week's rent.'

Jack looked wary. 'Oh, I don't think we could do that,' he said.

'Might?' Mrs Wickham said, ignoring Jack. 'You mean you'd settle for nineteen shillings and sixpence?'

'Well ...' Mr Thrush looked about to change his mind.

Before he could do so, Mrs Wickham was opening her handbag and taking out the keys.

'Sarah –' Jack began.

'I'm only doing what she's got to do sooner or later,' she snapped, handing over the keys to Mr Thrush. 'Besides,' she added, 'who's paying the money?'

22

Paula stood in the front drive, staring at the car piled with her belongings. Her mother was on one side of her, Uncle Jack on the other.

'You did what?' Paula said.

'You couldn't afford it,' Mrs Wickham said defensively. 'You owed two weeks' rent. Nearly three. I saved you from that. I've never owed a penny in my life.'

Paula moved closer to the car, her eyes wide with disbelief. 'You haven't.' She turned to Jack. 'She hasn't. How could you let her? It was my house! Our house! It – it – ' Her voice broke as she stared at the car. 'You *can't* have done it!'

Jack put his arm around her. 'Nay, love.' He squeezed her as he had done when she was a child and needed comforting. 'It's a shame that it had to happen like that, but it had to happen, and your mother was saving you money.'

Paula was still staring at her things in the car. 'Nine and ninepence,' she said. 'Did he give you the key money back?' She turned, watched her mother put a hand to her heart. 'No, he wouldn't, would he?'

Mrs Wickham found her voice. 'Key money?'

'That's how you get houses from that vulture,' Paula said. 'Richard gave him twenty pounds.'

'Twenty?' Mrs Wickham squeaked. 'Oh my God!'

Jack took his arm from round Paula and put it around Mrs Wickham.

'Nine and ninepence,' Paula said flatly. 'Nine and –'

She stopped, peered at the car, then turned to her mother and Jack. 'Where's the television receiver?'

They stood for a moment in silence, looking at her.

'You mean . . .' Jack cleared his throat '. . . the thing with valves?'

'Yes. The thing with valves.'

'That bit of junk,' Mrs Wickham scoffed. 'We sold it.'

Paula's eyes went wide again. 'You sold it?'

'To the totter,' her mother said. 'I paid your rent. I can't get all your stuff in here, can I?'

'That was Richard's,' Paula said.

'Well, there's not much he can do about it now, is there?'

Paula moved on her mother, fists clenched. Jack got between them. A neighbour hoeing his garden stopped to watch.

'How much did you get for it?' Paula demanded.

'Go inside,' Mrs Wickham ordered her.

'How much?'

'Making an exhibition of yourself,' Mrs Wickham hissed.

Paula's control dissolved. '*How much?*' she screamed.

'You're mad, Paula!'

'Yes, I am mad, yes!'

'For God's sake,' Mrs Wickham said 'Get her inside!'

The neighbour and a passer-by watched placidly as

Jack half coaxed and half bundled Paula into the hallway. Mrs Wickham hurried in behind them and slammed the door. Paula twisted away from Jack.

'How much?' she demanded. 'Go on. Tell me. How much?'

'Ninepence,' Jack said.

Paula leaned against the wall, shaking her head. 'Ninepence. You got ten shillings and three pence for twenty pounds. Where am I going to find twenty pounds again? Even if there were any houses!'

'You're living here,' Mrs Wickham said.

'That was my home, Mother!'

'You couldn't afford to keep it up!'

Jack glanced nervously at the trembling china ornaments on the shelf.

'I'd have managed!'

'How?' Mrs Wickham yelled.

'I don't know how!'

Paula clamped both hands to the top of her head and shut her eyes tightly, struggling to accommodate what was happening to her. She opened her eyes and glared at her mother.

'It's up to me to find out whether I can or not, not you! It was ours! His! And the television receiver was his. I don't care if people laughed at it and said it would never work. It was his. I wanted Carol to see it. It was his! I wanted her to see it!'

Mrs Wickham was not capable of admitting how upset she had become. 'What have I done?' She turned to Jack. 'If I knew what I'd done . . . We were getting on so well, so well . . .'

Both women were in a torment of confusion. They talked across each other, like blind swimmers casting about for something to hold on to.

'Getting on so well . . .' Mrs Wickham said, as close as she would ever come to tears.

'We were, we were,' Paula managed.

'Better than we have for years, years . . .'

'. . . But I never thought in a thousand years,' Paula said, 'you'd . . . you'd –'

'But if you keep going on like this, I can't stand it,' Mrs Wickham said, 'I can't go on having you here, really I can't . . .'

Paula heard that and closed her eyes for a moment, then she began to laugh. 'Oh Mother, Mother,' she said. 'Do you ever listen to yourself? Where do you expect me to go – now?'

After this there was some coming together, fragile but real. The baby interrupted their arguments: her demands became paramount. As the days grew warmer Mrs Wickham would sit with Carol in the garden, talking nonsense and feeling fulfilled by it. A central pleasure of being a grandmother, Mrs Wickham discovered, was that the baby could always be handed back to the care of her mother when she'd had enough. It was one case where you could have your cake and eat it.

From Paula's point of view the arrangement was nearly as pleasant, once she let herself accept it. She could not deny that Mrs Wickham was doing Carol good. Within days of moving to Moorland Road Paula sensed a difference: she thought of it as a gathering of the baby's qualities, a sharpening in her character.

Then one bright morning the peace of the house was shattered. A hammering on the front door was so abrupt and loud it made Mrs Wickham dribble tea down the front of her dressing-gown. She put down her cup, strode to the door and wrenched it open. Paula appeared at the top of the stairs. They both stared at the small figure on the doorstep. It was Bri Longman, with a bruised cheek. He had a rucksack with a broken strap slung on his shoulder. Tiger was at his heel.

'Our Bob's dead,' he said as abruptly as his knock. 'We got letter this morning.'

He turned to go then, leaving Mrs Wickham staring at him, mystified. Paula hurried down and called him back. She brought him in, the dog following with its ears flat, tail tucked in.

'Wait in there,' she said, prodding Bri into the front room.

She went to the kitchen, followed by Mrs Wickham, shuffling in her slippers to keep up. For a minute nothing was said. Mrs Wickham watched Paula put on the kettle, then get out a loaf and a pot of jam. Her face showed nothing. As she began slicing the bread Mrs Wickham spoke up.

'What's he come here for? He's nothing to do with you.' She frowned as Paula cut a doorstep from the loaf. 'Not so thick!'

'He comes from Mafeking Park,' Paula said, cutting another substantial slice.

'You hated his brother. For good reason.'

Paula jerked her head at the hallway. 'He didn't, did he?' She began spreading jam on the bread in a way that made her mother wince.

Five minutes later, as Bri continued to look round the front room in awe, Paula came in carrying a tray with bread and jam and tea. Her mother was behind her, eyeing Bri and his dog with open distrust. Paula put down the tray. Bri looked round.

'He said it were a palace,' he said.

Paula pointed at the tray, indicating he should help himself. She sat down. 'What did the letter say?'

'I don't know.' Bri shook his head violently. 'Vera wouldn't read it out again. Killed. On duty. Something.' He set his mouth. 'Bitch,' he said. 'I'm not never going back there again. Never.' He picked up a piece of bread and jam and sank his teeth into it.

'Watch the carpet,' Mrs Wickham said.

'What happened?' Paula asked Bri.

He swallowed. 'Vera said good riddance to bad rubbish.'

'She didn't.'

'She did!' Bri insisted, tears brimming. 'She did! She put money on the table, she said go on go and get drunk, to me Mam she did. She said you're going to get drunk so you may as well do it now. I'm not going to drink until he comes back me Mam said – he's not coming back you fool she said, don't you understand?'

He was chewing steadily into the bread and jam as though it might be taken from him at any moment. Jam was building up steadily around his mouth and on his fingers. The dog was watching him fixedly. So was Mrs Wickham.

'Watch the carpet,' she said

'There's Vera in a dead state because me Mam wouldn't go for a drink, when half the time she used to be trying to drag her out of the Blue – I don't understand –'

'Watch the –'

Paula slipped a plate under a blob of jam just as it dropped. Oblivious, Bri carried on, the words streaming out of him.

'Then she said he was rubbish and I cracked her one before she brayed me. I'm not going back there. *He* used to go off. He did. Bob. My brother.'

Bri gripped his rucksack between his knees and picked up the second piece of bread and jam while he was still chewing the final mouthful of the first.

'Use a plate, Bri,' Paula said.

He pointed to his cheek. 'Have I got a bruise?'

'Yes,' Mrs Wickham said.

'You should see hers.' He bit the fresh piece of bread and chewed with starved satisfaction. 'Do you think he was rubbish?' he asked Paula.

'No,' she said, 'no. I don't think he was rubbish. I don't think Vera meant that.'

'She said it! What did she mean then?'

'She meant . . .' Paula shrugged. 'Well, I don't know, she's kept the place going, done all the work, and somehow he's . . . he was the sort of person who . . .'

Bri blinked at her. 'What?'

She sat twisting her fingers, unable to say any more.

Bri stared at her. The bread, unheeded now, began slipping from his fingers. Tiger had his head cocked, waiting for it to fall. The final half-inch was sliding from his grip when Mrs Wickham snatched it from him and put it on a plate. She stood shaking her jam-stained fingers with disgust. Bri didn't notice, he was too intent on Paula.

'Are you sad?' he asked her.

'Yes.'

'You don't look it. I thought you'd cry. You had his baby.'

Paula stood up quickly, emotional suddenly, catching a stony look from her mother. She did not trust herself to speak, so she went out into the hall. Mrs Wickham followed her, still holding the plate.

'I don't know what's going on!' she said, staring at Paula. 'What to believe!'

'Do you think I do?' Paula said, heading for the stairs.

As Mrs Wickham turned back to the front room she nearly collided with Bri and the dog.

'Can he have that?' Bri said, pointing at the piece of bread and jam on the plate.

'Dogs don't eat jam and bread.'

'He does,' Bri said indignantly. 'It's all he does eat.'

In her room Paula looked for a moment at the flowers blooming down where the shelter had been. The baby was awake, making soft throaty sounds, talking to her mother. Paula smiled mechanically at her as she opened a dressing-table drawer and took out a wad of papers. She spread them between her hands, all of them identical except for the dates, money orders with her name on them in Bob's round, careful, childish handwriting. She had burnt his letters but there was sufficient of her mother in her to make her unable to burn money.

She folded the orders into her handbag, hearing his voice: *That's the secret. That's magic. I can do anything* . . .

Down in the kitchen the dog was still licking the plate, even though every trace of bread and jam had gone. Paula, wearing her outdoor coat, came in carrying the baby. Her mother turned to her.

'You don't have much luck, do you?'

Paula burst out laughing.

'What's wrong now? What have I said?'

'It's how you put it, Mother. You should be on Tommy Handley.' She held out Carol, who smiled at Mrs Wickham. 'Go to your grandma. I think I've got that right, at least.'

Mrs Wickham took the baby. 'Where are you going?'

'There and back, to see how far it is.' Paula kissed Carol's cheek. 'Don't sell her, will you?'

23

The sky was cloudless as Paula and Bri went through the gate with Tiger behind them. It felt as if it would be a warm day. Bri asked where they were going.

'We're going to do a Bob,' Paula told him.

'What? Bugger off?'

Paula could not make herself laugh at that. 'There was another side to him,' she said.

Bri nodded, very seriously. The gesture had an abrupt earnestness that mirrored Bob's way of nodding. Paula caught the similarity with a shock. She had to turn away and walk on quickly, gathering herself. Bri paused, whistled for the dog, then ran to catch up with her. Without hesitating, he slipped his hand into hers. Paula closed her fingers tightly around his.

When they reached Queen's Square the electioneering was in full swing. Paula saw Penny Winter on a platform splashed with Conservative and Unionist posters, with pictures of Winston Churchill pasted beside photographs of Seaforth's Conservative candidate, Major Ralph Wallace. At the other side of the square Fred Spence was on the back of a lorry stuck with Labour posters. Pictures of Clement Attlee were juxtaposed with photographs of Jim Henshaw, the local Labour candidate.

'The war has been won not by one man, but by the people!' Fred told the little crowd by the side of the lorry. He looked earnestly into the middle distance, as if he were addressing thousands. 'We were cheated before! Don't let the men be cheated when they come home this time! Vote Labour and we *will* build the Homes for Heroes!'

At the same time Penny was delivering the message from the other camp. She did it with less vigour than Fred, but with a great deal more charm. 'The man who led you to victory will lead you to peace!' she cried. 'All the Socialists will build is more bureaucracy and more rationing! We will get people back to work! Reconstructing the economy first means we will be able to *afford* the homes for you to live in!'

During Penny's speech Paula came out of the Post Office and haltingly approached the offices of Scawton Estates, her courage dipping as she curled her fingers around the handle of the door. She hesitated a moment, staring at the gilded lettering on the glass panel, getting back her resentment and the confidence to drive it. Behind her Bri launched an aeroplane he had made from a Labour leaflet. He groaned in disgust as it nose-dived.

Paula went inside, closing the door quietly behind her.

The air in the office smelt of beeswax with a dull trace of cigar smoke. Mr Thrush's desk sat near the door, on an area of floor covered with shiny linoleum. Row upon row of house keys hung on a board behind the desk, aligned to the rows of street names written in

Mr Thrush's copperplate hand. A few feet behind the desk the carpet began, rich brown Yorkshire wool stretching back towards an inner office, from which deep, serious voices murmured.

Paula approached the desk, her bag clutched deferentially between her hands. Mr Thrush looked up. Outside young Bri's voice could be heard, yelling boyish commentary to the election speeches as he threw his aeroplane around.

Paula explained her business. She wanted to take possession of the keys to number 15 Roberts Avenue again, and was in a position to pay the outstanding amount of rent. She opened her bag and took out some money.

'I'm sorry, Mrs Austen,' Mr Thrush said coldly, 'but you are no longer the tenant of that property.'

'But I can pay this week in full! And the next!'

Bri came in with Tiger and stood beside Paula.

'I'm afraid there's nothing I can do,' Mr Thrush was saying. 'You ended the tenancy.'

'My mother did!'

'On your behalf,' Mr Thrush added smoothly. 'I'm sorry.'

Bri launched his aircraft across the office. Tiger ran after it.

'It's still empty!' Paula said, feeling the beginning of despair. She pointed at the board. 'The key's there!'

Bri saw exactly where she was pointing – there were no other keys near it. At the same moment Mr Thrush rose from his seat and glared at the boy.

'Take that dog out of here!'

Mr Thrush came round the desk. As he did, Bri wriggled under it, grabbed the key and thrust it into Paula's hand.

'Run for it!'

Bri leapt to the door and pulled it open. Paula stared at him, transfixed. Mr Thrush strode across to the door, slammed it shut and bolted it.

'Aw, bloody hell!' Bri yelled at Paula. 'Once you're in the bastards can't get you out!'

Tiger, an old enemy of Mr Thrush, had now gone for him, barking and snapping at his legs. Bri called the dog off and stared sullenly towards the carpeted area of the office. Paula looked. A tall distinguished-looking man in his late sixties with unwavering brown eyes was standing there, watching them. He wore the most perfectly cut suit Paula had ever seen, and his air of authority seemed similarly unflawed. The entire place was silent now, only the electioneering noises from outside penetrating faintly as the man went on staring.

'Repossessed tenant, Lord Scawton,' Mr Thrush said. 'Trying to get her keys back.'

'Put them down,' Lord Scawton told Paula.

She did as he said.

'Get out.'

Paula's anger began to boil up, but as Mr Thrush unbolted the door and opened it, she turned to leave. Lord Scawton narrowed his eyes for a second. 'Haven't I seen you before?'

Paula looked at him and nodded. 'At dinner,' she said.

He looked astonished. 'Dinner?'

'I served you at dinner, sir.'

She had tried to catch the 'sir' before it leapt out, but she was too late.

'Ah!' Lord Scawton's face cleared and he almost smiled. 'At the Winters'.'

'Yes, sir.'

'Well . . .' He shrugged, making a regretful mouth, turning to go back to his office. 'There's nothing I can do. You shouldn't fall behind with your rent.'

'Two weeks,' Paula said bitterly.

Lord Scawton stopped. He turned. 'We take no action for a month.'

By the door Bri shrugged and jerked his head towards Mr Thrush. 'After the key money, isn't he?'

'Out, you!' Thrush shouted, blushing scarlet, shoving Bri outside.

Lord Scawton came forward, frowning. He looked at the open ledger on Mr Thrush's desk.

Three minutes later Paula emerged triumphantly from the office. Bri had been watching the electioneers packing up. As he turned and saw Paula she held up the keys to number 15 Roberts Avenue.

'It worked!' Bri yelled, delighted. 'It worked!' He jumped for sheer pleasure and jerked his fist in the air. 'One for Bob and one for thee!'

Paula tried to make a similar gesture and was suddenly overcome. She turned away. Bri ran forward and put his arms around her. They held each other very tightly.

24

On a windy Friday evening, an hour after it had turned dark, a man stopped at the front gate of Mrs Wickham's house on Moorland Road. He stood for a moment, looking up and down the street, then eased up the catch on the gate.

Inside the house, in the front room, Jack was reading the paper while his wife, Enid, watched Mrs Wickham sew a black collar on to a dress. The white collar she had removed lay on the table beside her.

'Nobody sews a stitch like you, Sarah,' Enid said.

'I wish she appreciated that,' Mrs Wickham sighed.

'She will, love.'

'Aye.' Mrs Wickham stabbed the needle through the fabric and pulled the thread taut. 'At my funeral.'

There was a sharp click from outside, the sound of the gate catch. Mrs Wickham got out of her chair with a grunt. She pushed back the curtain and peered out, her face close to the glass. The path was empty. She watched for a moment, seeing the wind rustling the bushes and blowing scraps of paper about, then she went back to her chair. For a moment she stared at her sewing, lips pursed.

'Her old servant's dress,' she said. 'For Richard's funeral . . .'

'Nobody will know,' Jack said.

She looked at him. '*I* know, Jack! *I* know! It's not just a funeral, it's a *memorial service*! Eight widows and she'll be the only one wearing a made-up servant's dress!' A wave of despair crossed her face, leaving her mouth free to quiver a second before she tightened it again. 'She refuses everything. I thought for a minute, when she was here – I don't know ... She'll soon be thrown out of that slum and she won't come back here. What went wrong? What happened?'

It had been two months since Paula went back to Roberts Avenue. The last time Mrs Wickham had visited her the place had looked poorer and the furnishings were more sparse than ever. Even the threadbare scrap of rug had gone from the back room. Everything that could be sold had been disposed of, except for the silly electrical thing Richard had been working on, that Paula had bought back from Jacko, to whom the totter had sold it. It stood on its table again, half finished, several valves broken on its journey to Jacko and back.

Mrs Wickham finished the last stitch, looped the cotton and pulled it tight. She bit the thread and stared at the dress on her lap, aware this was a summation, the conclusion of a long line of such chores. She stood up abruptly and thrust the dress at Enid.

'Take it to her, will you? Try it on her.'

Enid folded the dress. She looked troubled. 'You know my fingers are all thumbs, Sarah. What if it doesn't ...'

She stopped, shocked to see Mrs Wickham, the woman of implacable principle and granite will, blinking back tears. The moment was so brief it might not have happened. Mrs Wickham picked up the tea-tray, gripping it like a lifeline.

'It'll fit,' she said as she hurried from the room.

At the kitchen door she balanced the tray on one hand as she reached with the other for the light switch. At that moment an instinct, an awareness of a presence, made her stop. She looked through the window into the garden, which was just visible in the dim light from the street lamps. Seeing something, she moved closer to the back window.

In the front room Jack and Enid were gathering their things together, preparing to leave, when they heard the crash of breaking china from the kitchen. They rushed out and found Mrs Wickham standing in the middle of the kitchen floor, the light on now, the tray and the shattered remains of the tea things scattered across the floor. Her eyes were wide, the pupils dilated as she pointed at the back window.

'Someone, something . . .'

Jack and Enid ran out into the garden. There was no one in sight. The only sound was a passing car. Enid went back into the house as Jack walked further down the garden, bending low over the new flower-bed where the shelter had been.

Enid cleared up the mess. Mrs Wickham watched her from a chair, too shocked to stand up.

'I swear it was him,' she said, 'his ghost . . .'

Jack came striding in, making her jump.

'Ghost?' he said. 'It was something a bit more solid than a ghost that trod on those flowers.'

A short time later, over at Mafeking Park, the lights were still on behind the closed sign on Jacko's shop door, and Jacko could be seen cutting a slice of cake. Tiger lay on the pavement outside the shop, his chin down on his paws. As he waited his ears pricked suddenly. He stood up and padded around uneasily, looking towards the ginnel. He began to whine deep in the back of his throat. The whine got louder as Bri came out of the shop, carrying the piece of cake.

'All right, all right.'

He tore off a lump of cake and was about to lob it when Tiger turned and ran off into the darkness of the ginnel, barking frantically.

Bri ran after him. 'What is it?' he called. 'What have you found?'

As he reached the ginnel he stopped abruptly, seeing a shadowy figure standing just ahead. He took a step closer, careful, ready to run, his eyes adjusting to the weak lamplight in the gloom. He looked upward and gasped. He was staring into Bob's face.

An old man was walking past as Bri opened his mouth to scream. Bob clamped his hand over the boy's mouth and drew him bodily into the darkness of the ginnel. The dog was silenced, too, as Bob made an instantly recalled spurning movement with his shoe. Tiger whimpered.

Now Bri found he was moving at speed, his body held, his legs weak but running as the upper part of him was dragged along, away from the curiosity of any passer-by. He was released then to run alongside, the wind whipping at the pair of them as they ran on out of Kitchener Street and across the bomb site, the dog pacing them.

They dropped down, panting, at the place where Bob had slept the night before he gave himself up. It was a minute before either one had control of his breathing. The dog lay a couple of yards away.

Bri and Bob stared at one another as their breathing settled. Bri was still clutching the slab of cake, unaware of it as he stared wide-eyed at his brother's face.

'Are you alive?'

He was still for a moment, as if he wasn't sure. Then he grinned. 'Feel,' he said.

Bri touched his arm, squeezed it. Bob reached out and closed his own fingers warmly on the boy's shoulder.

'I never thought . . .' the words stuck.

'What?' Bri said.

Bob drew him close and hugged him. '. . . I'd be that glad to see you! You little villain!'

Tiger came snuffling close and Bob hugged him too, then shoved him away. 'Flea-ridden bloody mongrel!' He turned and grasped Bri's hand and held it up, staring at the cake. 'You thieving bastard!' He measured the cake with his finger. 'He robbed you, Bri. He allus gives you more cake when he robs you.'

'I gorra quid,' Bri said excitedly. He held up the folded note. 'Look!'

'For what?'

'Canteen. Fish knives and forks.'

Bob prepared a scornful curl of the lip, then saw the look on Bri's face and let his expression soften. 'Ah, well, not bad, not bad.'

Bri's back stiffened with the approval. He broke the cake and offered Bob a piece. Bob took it and went to sit on a broken section of wall. They ate, Bri coming closer and sitting beside his brother.

'It's the same cake,' Bob said, chewing. 'Stale as old Nick, been in that tin since I left!'

Bri was staring, still unable to believe it. 'They found your body,' he said.

Bob stopped eating. He spat the chewed cake into his hand and threw it away, shuddering with disgust.

'Let's go home,' Bri said. 'Me Mam'll –'

Bob grabbed him by the front of his cardigan and drew him forward violently.

'Home? If you tell her, if you tell that cow . . .' His voice was harsh, his breath hot on Bri's ear. 'If you tell anyone . . . I'm dead, you understand?'

Bri was terrified. Did he mean he *was* dead? Or pretending to be? To make it worse, the figure held up his hand in their old sign of comradeship.

'Are you with me?'

Bri was not sure that he was, but he raised his hand half-way.

'Till death?' Bob said.

'Till death.' Bri lowered his hand, afraid to ask for an explanation, but desperate for one. 'They said you went after a prisoner . . .' He shrank back as Bob came close again, but this time he took hold of Bri gently, by the shoulders, looking straight into his face.

'Aye,' he said softly. 'He told me he had treasure.'

Bri's eyes widened. 'Did he?'

'He tricked me . . .'

223

The entire drama could play itself out in seconds now, Bob had recalled it so often, but its impact was always the same, it reminded him how easy it was to make things change, if you took a big enough gamble.

The memory rushed through him. He had never been so close to being deliberately killed, he would never be closer. He could still see Karl von Berner bring down the piece of timber on his skull, could still feel the sensation of heaviness, hear the noise in his head as the forest tilted back and he saw the sky rimmed with leaves, then darkness.

He recalled the swimming light as he came round, seeing von Berner putting on his Corporal's uniform, buttoning the jacket. The gun was a few feet from Bob's face, lying in the dirt. For a moment Bob's nerves would not respond, he ordered his hand to move and nothing happened. Then pain came, swamping his head, and with it he regained movement. He reached for the gun, hearing the voices of the other two soldiers, Midge and Geoff, still some distance away. As his fingers touched the gun von Berner turned and saw him.

He jumped on Bob and they struggled. Bob had the gun but the other man's weight was on that arm. He tried to shout to the others but von Berner put a hand over his mouth. The heel of the hand stayed clamped on his lips as the fingers inched round, clawing upwards, going for his eyes.

Bob brought up his knee sharply, slamming his thigh into von Berner's crotch. The German reared up with the pain. Bob's hand was suddenly free. He banged the gun against the side of von Berner's head, then on the top, over and over, frantically, until the German fell over. Even then Bob sat up, following him, continuing to beat his skull with the steel gun barrel.

Then something occurred to him and his hand stopped in mid-air. He shook von Berner and turned him over. The head came round, the lifeless eyes staring up at Bob. He turned away, shocked, trying to think. Scrambling across the ground he picked up the German's jacket and went through the pockets. They were empty. He shook the lifeless body again, stared at the waxy face.

'Where's the money?' He stared around the clearing, shaking with bitter interior laughter. 'Where is it?'

He stood up slowly and glimpsed Midge and Geoff in the distance. They disappeared again in the thickness of shrubbery. Bob put his hands to his mouth to shout to them, then a thought hit him like a hammer.

He stared down at the bloody head above the Corporal's stripes. It could have been his dead body. The thought hit him like another blow — it could *be* his dead body! A sound made him duck down. Geoff had suddenly reappeared, twenty feet away. If he had turned a fraction to his right he would have seen Bob. But he turned the other way. By the time he did look in Bob's direction, Bob was no longer visible.

He crouched by the body, looking at it, feeling himself seized with an odd intensity of feeling as he thought of Paula, of getting back to England. After all, he had never really been a Corporal. He was something very much more – or something very much less. He adjusted his grip on the bloodstained gun and put the barrel to the back of von Berner's battered skull. The explosion, when it came, was no more than a thump. Bob had been caught up in the memory for no more than seconds, but Bri was staring at him, and Bob realized he had put his hands over his ears, trying to cut out the sound of the gun.

'Did you find the treasure?' Bri said.

Bob looked at him a long moment, bringing himself back. 'Oh. Aye. Aye. When I got back to London, eventually. Fish knives? Streets are paved with them there.'

He stuck his hand in his inside pocket and brought out a bundle of notes. There wasn't all that much but rolling it in a wad made it seem more. He'd quarrelled with the people he'd been doing black market jobs with – petrol coupons, clothing. The money had been going down, and the problems rising, so when he'd heard, from someone who came from Seaforth, about the memorial service . . .

He peeled off a pound from the thinning wad. 'Thanks!' Bri gasped, awestruck. 'Thanks!' He stuffed the note in his pocket with the other one.

'And the women in London,' Bob said. 'You should see the women.' He lit a cigarette and blew out a narrow stream of smoke.

'Did you come back to see her?' Bri said.

'Her?' Bob laughed. 'I came back because I heard they were burying me! With honours! I couldn't resist it.'

'She cried.'

'What?'

'When she heard you were dead.'

'Aye, with joy. I can see her. I can just see her.' He could. He could see her satisfaction. He remembered every word, every punctuation mark of her letter.

'She pretended she weren't upset, like you do, you know, but when I said well you had his baby she looked ready to weep buckets and got your money orders and said she were going to do a Bob . . .' Bri took a breath as Bob, forgetting to be casual, leaned forward, staring intently. '. . . She did, because she couldn't pay her rent, because he's dead and we went to that bugger Thrush and –'

'Hang on, hang on! Who's dead?'

'Her husband,' Bri said, as if everybody knew that.

Mrs Wickham had gone along to Paula's after all because she did not want to be left in the house alone, not after what she had seen, or thought she had seen, in the garden.

There were not enough chairs at Roberts Avenue. Jack stood, while Mrs Wickham sat in a chair near the door, staring bleakly as Enid helped Paula into the black dress.

The calmest of the lot. Nothing more, she believed, could happen to her. She had coped with the worst and survived. She could even make a joke about her mother's snobbery.

'You've always wanted me to be a servant again, Mother.'

That didn't go down well.

Enid fussed about behind Paula and did up the dress at the back. She knew it was right as soon as Enid put the hook into the eye. And ironically, although her mother refused to see it, its very simplicity made it right.

'It fits perfectly, Mother,' Paula said. 'Thank you.'

'Of course it fits perfectly,' Mrs Wickham said acidly. 'It doesn't make it any less cheap.'

There was a knock at the door. Bob heard the sounds in the house and, after all this, stupidly wanted to run. He suddenly didn't believe what Bri had said. He would rather be back in Germany than face Paula. She was opening the door . . .

There stood the last person in the world he expected to see. Mrs Wickham. In the confused background was someone in a black dress, Paula, turning to see who it was.

The audience was there and waiting. The drive to convince them was strong. Bob stood in the little room and gave the performance of his life, gaining confidence by the second, inducing belief in every word he said. His gaze moved from Jack to Enid to Paula as he spoke, but he directed his story with particular strength at Mrs Wickham, who looked mesmerized.

'Mistaken identity,' he said. 'Very easily done in the thick of battle. I got one here.' He pointed to where his head had been scarred. 'I woke up in hospital not knowing who I was, where I'd come from . . .'

Paula stared at him. 'But your memory's come back now,' she said.

He looked at her, his eyes softening. 'Yes.' He moved towards her. 'It's coming back now. Yes. Yes . . .'

'You're lying,' she said, and turned to her mother. 'Don't listen to him.'

Bob looked at the others, making a show of bewilderment. He gave Paula a small puzzled smile.

'You're lying, aren't you?' she said, her eyes steady on his, a hardness in her voice he had not heard before. The spell could not survive the chill. Abruptly the pretence was gone. Bob sagged.

'Paula –'

'Go away,' she said.

'Bri said –'

'Go away,' she told him again. 'Just go!'

Disenchantment had struck Mrs Wickham swiftly. She was up off her chair, glaring at Bob. 'Your memory's come back, has it? You remember me? You remember when you were Mrs Winter's chauffeur? Do you remember that night? Do you?'

Bob moved back as she closed on him.

'Don't interfere, Mother,' Paula said.

'Don't interfere?' Mrs Wickham was incensed. 'My God! I'll interfere! After what he's done to you I'll inter–'

'Stop it!' Paula shouted. 'Stop it! Will you all go away!'

Bob put out his hand and touched Paula. She jerked away as if she had been burned.

'I'll tell you,' he began, but Paula's anger boiled over, swamping his words.

'I don't *want* you to tell me!' she yelled. 'I don't

need you to tell me that you're a liar, a cheat and a thief! What else is there to know? Even your being dead is a lie! My memory must have gone! How could I have forgotten what you're like? You're on the run again, aren't you? Are you going to lie again? You are, aren't you?'

Upstairs the baby began to cry. Bob heard her and looked at Paula as she moved to the stairs. He grabbed her.

'I went on the run for you, you bitch!' he snarled.

'Get the police!' Mrs Wickham howled.

As Enid opened the door Bob kicked it shut.

'Come on, son,' Jack said, trying a different tack.

'Don't you "son" me, you stupid old fart!'

Paula twisted away and Bob grabbed her again. Jack tried to pull him off. Mrs Wickham picked up a spindly chair.

Out on the street young Bri stopped abruptly, eyes wide as he heard the shouting and clattering from number 15. The door flew open suddenly and Bob hurtled out, did a swift turn and ran past Bri down the road.

'Get him!' Jack shouted at a passer-by. 'Get the police!'

Bob staggered in the shadows as the passer-by tried to trip him.

'There's another one of them!' Enid screeched, pointing at Bri as he turned to run after Bob.

Jack took hold of Bri and dragged him into the house. The boy stood blinking in the light, awestruck at the signs of chaos and destruction. Mrs Wickham stood by a broken chair, visibly shaking, a look of outrage on her face.

'Dead!' she said, finding her voice. 'I shall never believe he's dead until I see him nailed down and buried!'

25

The church stood prominently apart, overlooking Seaforth and, by unforeseeable misfortune, directly facing the upward draught of smoke from the factories and mills. It was doubly unfortunate that where the church had been built, the funnelling air from the Leathdale Valley slowed and spread out, so that smoke hung permanently around the building and invaded the aisles, creating a misty effect marred by faint but tenacious industrial smells.

That day great care had been taken to present the church in its best light. Brasses had been shined, pews were polished and the gilt of the lectern had a lustre that was possible only with old and cherished metalwork. Hymnbooks were stacked at the ends of the rows of pews and the hymn numbers were posted ready in the slats. There were flowers on the altar, and ten new names had been painted in bright gilt letters on the memorial plaque on the west aisle. The seventh name was Robert Longman.

Everyone was dressed up for the memorial service. Sal Longman, aware by now that she still had an elder son, had taken a few drinks to celebrate and to fortify herself for the ceremony. Vera, Bri and Dora walked a little apart from her and were followed inside by Dick

Moxham, his barmaid Sue, Miss Thwaites and Mrs Thomas. Fred Spence walked beside his wife and his son Arthur, who was in uniform.

Penny Winter got out of a car helped by her husband, Andrew, in his Lieutenant-Colonel's uniform. Near by, Mrs Wickham, splendid in black, walked along the drive with Paula, who was carrying Carol. As Penny Winter stopped to express her sympathy to Paula, Mrs Wickham gave the collar of Paula's dress an apologetic twitch.

Inside, an urgent whispered discussion was taking place between the Bishop and Lord Scawton. Mr Thrush, who was the verger, stood listening to them, a variety of fawning expressions passing across his face. Finally the Bishop turned to Mr Thrush and muttered something behind his hand. Thrush in his turn summoned two workmen to put black tape over the name Robert Longman on the commemorative plaque on the west aisle.

Sal Longman saw what was happening and began to laugh hysterically. The laughter spread to Bri, who began to choke with it and was told to shut up by Vera, between her efforts to control Sal. 'I don't know which of you is worst,' she hissed.

Whispers began at the back and spread to the front of the church, where the Winters sat with Penny's sister, Diana, and her husband John Stacey. Diana, a woman who managed to make mourning look fashionable, appeared to be bored and restless. Outside, Bob heard the service begin. He had spent the night on a bomb site: life was rapidly returning to normal. Now he walked through the churchyard, seemingly idly, hands in his pockets, threading his way between the gravestones. He had no idea what he was going to do, but it struck him, with great force, that although those in the church would have jeered at him if he'd said it, this *was* his memorial service.

Something was being buried, if not someone.

They were singing. He had always liked hymns, even if the words were stupid. Lump in the throat stuff.

He wasn't going in the church, was he? That would be downright stupid. The Army was in there. His old mates the Redcaps. Ready to cart him off to the glasshouse. But wasn't the church a sanctuary?

Was he going into the church or going to have a last look at her?

The singing was louder. Just in the porch. Perhaps he could see her from there. No. He'd have to go a bit further. A Redcap had seen him. San Fairy Ann. In for a penny. What did it matter?

One of the Redcaps was starting to move towards him but had been stopped by another. This was holy ground. There was that drunken bag Sal! His mother. His family. He had to join them! He just had to do this!

They were all round him, kissing him, hugging him. This was ridiculous! He wasn't crying, was he?

There she was. Paula. Her back towards him. Nothing but her back. But he thought in a crazy way – at least I've seen her back. Daft, bloody insane he was about her – he might as well admit it. What was that old prat at the front saying?

'They are not dead but sleep,' the Bishop said, 'and we pray for them in the sure and certain knowledge of the life to come. We pray for Richard Austen . . .'

Paula's head lowered at his name, she drew Carol closer and her eyes shut tightly.

'. . . For David Baker, Michael Crowther, George Edwards, Brian Gough, David King . . .' The Bishop hesitated as his eye encountered the deletion. '. . . William Lucas, Paul Osborne, Ronald Spence . . .'

Arthur Spence swallowed and his father tightened his grip on Mrs Spence's hand at the mention of her other son's name.

Further down the church, Bob knelt with his eyes shut, opening them only a couple of times to glance across at Paula.

Later, as Mr Thrush and a sidesman took the collection, Bob looked round and saw that the Redcaps were now standing by the door. He looked across at Paula again; she still appeared to be in a world of her own.

He knew what he was going to do now. Everything was clear. Settled. Outside the church he greeted the Redcaps like old friends. He promised not to make a fuss if they would let him do one thing. One thing only.

Paula was watching him now. She expected him to come to her. He didn't. She saw Bob speak to Mr Thrush, then Thrush looked towards her. Bob took a bundle of banknotes from his pocket and handed them to Thrush. She realized suddenly what he was doing and ran towards the group.

'No!' she shouted, making people turn and stare.

'*No!*' She stopped in front of Bob. The Redcaps moved protectively close to him. Paula and Bob stared at one another.

'It's no use,' she said, the words a cry of pain. 'No use.'

He knew that, but he repeated the words idiotically. 'No use?'

Suddenly she was kissing him. Holding him. She didn't care either. They were both completely unaware of the speechless crowd round them. The only sound was from young Carol, wriggling in her grandmother's arms, calling for her mother and, for once, being ignored. Sal moved across and whispered something to Mrs Wickham. Confused and appalled, she handed over the baby without realizing who was taking her. The child's crying seemed to bring the entire gathering back to reality. People moved and began talking again.

A Redcap tapped Bob on the shoulder. He nodded and stepped away from Paula, keeping his eyes on hers as long as he could. Then he turned and walked away between the two soldiers. They had gone five yards when he stopped abruptly and turned. The Redcaps tensed. Bob looked at Paula, and at Carol behind her in Sal's arms.

'I shall want her to take my name,' he said.

Then, before she could answer, he turned away and walked off smartly, flanked by his escort.